RUN RABBIT RUN

N. A. WILLIAMS

"You'd be surprised at the things you find when you go looking."

—Dr. Richard Powell

The Void

CHAPTER 1

SIXTEEN. IN LESS THAN TWENTY-FOUR hours, he would be sixteen years old. What did that even mean to a boy? He knew for a girl turning sixteen meant a whole lot. To girls, sixteen was a big deal. A *huge* deal. So huge their parents throw sweet sixteen celebrations: a kind of superficial rite of passage into womanhood that meant something and absolutely nothing at the same time.

For his classmate, Jessica Green, the *something* had been the no-boys-allowed party thrown at her parents' expense and the wish fulfillment of another pony added to a collection of preexisting ponies. The *nothing* part was claiming adulthood with none of the associated responsibilities.

For his friend Kyle Blum, who he met online through VRChat a year ago, thirteen had been his sixteen. The way he explained it was a bit complicated, but August got the overall picture. In the Jewish faith, when a boy reaches age thirteen, he goes through a ritual called bar mitzvah. The ritual symbolizes a boy becoming responsible for his actions, and the father no longer punished for his son's sins.

August wasn't Jewish. Far as he knew, his family didn't subscribe to any religious faith. That wasn't to say they were atheists. He didn't believe that. The topic of religion simply had never come up in their house. His only experience with the house of God had come from his short-lived stay at St Anthony's, a boarding school for boys. This was before his body started to undergo its unfortunate change.

Lying on his back in the made bed, he stared up at the white rabbit clutched in his hands. The stuffed animal's red glass eyes stared back at him. *Sixteen*, he thought. For him turning sixteen marked another year of survival. Another year of proving the doctors wrong. Another year of having enough strength in his legs and in his hands to walk and grip things.

In some ways, August's condition made him old. Made him more cognizant and appreciative when it came to the little things. Such as anticipating the next big superhero movie, watching television with his grandfather, or listening to his mother sing whenever the woman was clearheaded enough to do so.

Being self-aware wasn't without its downsides. Sleep was finding him less and less, and as a result, he was shrinking. In a month, he had gone from a size medium to small. He was scared. Had been scared for a while, but now he was really scared. August had accepted that he could very well close his eyes one night and never open them again. What frightened him was the shrinking. The possibility of fading, wasting away into some unrecognizable and helpless thing.

"If you think you're going to remain cooped up indoors like some hermit for the next three days, you've got another thing coming, young master." A stern voice invaded the bedroom. The three days remaining were part of August's five-day forced exile from the United Kingdom to the States. One day dedicated as a rest day (for all the good that had done the sleepless teen) and the second day dedicated to unpacking what the manservant deemed *the necessary things*. Now the third day, August assumed he was about to be persuaded again to do something productive.

"Is that so?" He said. No longer able to fight the burning fatigue in his arms, August lowered the rabbit to his chest. Before retiring to the bed, he had been busily unpacking his belongings in a bedroom larger than most people's apartments. The number of boxes were few. The majority of which had been shipped from overseas prior to their arrival. For this reason, the manservant's back was spared from doing any heavy lifting. The one exception was August's satchel. In it, he carried a top-of-the-line laptop, along with its many accessories. The device was a critical component in the way he interacted with the world while on the go.

While most boys his age were playing sports and experiencing girls for the first time, he occupied his mind by deep diving into computer hacking. The boxes on the floor spoke volumes about his interests. Some contained books ranging from computer exploitation to fashion. Others held carefully packaged comic books and vintage music posters. One poster in particular—unrolled—was of the '90s grunge band Breaching the Firmament.

"It is." The manservant said. "I've taken the liberty of putting together appropriate outdoor attire for you. You see, it's quite cold, and there's no telling how long we will be out for." Reginald Ristil stood six foot three inches tall. Not having entered the room, his broad shoulders made the doorway impassable, and there was an expectant look in his brown eyes. August recognized it and knew the man's mind was set in stone, whether he protested or not. He did not particularly mind the monkey wrench thrown in his plans to lose himself in daydreams, but for the life of him didn't understand the man's sudden declaration for them to venture out at such an ungodly hour. The sun had yet to rise.

"Then I suppose I best get dressed," August said, still wearing his pajamas. He rolled onto his side facing the manservant and, with some difficulty, sat up. Reginald did not rush to his aid. He was one of the few people in his life who did not treat him delicately. He was glad. If it were anyone else other than Reginald standing in the doorway, he would've been deeply embarrassed to be seen in clothes that did little to contribute to his size. His father would have avoided direct eye contact at all cost, and his mother would have scowled him for not notifying anyone that he needed to get up.

He was one-hundred percent aware of his condition and one-hundred percent aware that he did not stack up to the physicality of the average fifteen-year-old boy. He was small and progressively getting smaller, appearing closer to thirteen than he did his actual age, and preferred not to be seen unless fully dressed.

"Oh yes, I suppose you should," Reginald said, entering the room. He placed an armful of folded clothing onto the bed. "While you do, I'll finish making the preparations. Do come downstairs once you're ready."

"May I at least know where we're going?" August reached for the crutches leaned against the bed. He slipped an arm in one cuff, then the other, and lifted himself with practiced ease.

"Ah, I see you've found your mother's gift," Reginald said as if not hearing the question. The manservant picked up the toy rabbit. From a distance, it could pass as the real thing.

"My mother still thinks I'm a child. You'd be doing me a favor by tossing it in the bin."

"And upset the misses? I think not." Reginald declined. "Besides, it's a cute rabbit, wouldn't you agree?"

August's face darkened. He did *not* agree. His mother's constant childish gifts were smothering and borderline insulting. It was now his turn to ignore the manservant. "You haven't answered my question."

Reginald sighed. He should have known better than to try distracting the teen. Returning the rabbit to its resting place, he stood upright. "Hm, no. I don't think so. You'll just have to wait and see."

August glowered disapprovingly. While he did not mind the man derailing his initial plans (which, again, was to do nothing), he absolutely detested surprises.

Unphased by this, Reginald took his leave.

August turned his gaze towards the bed and studied the thick winter clothing left for him. *What are you up to old man?*

CHAPTER 2

FORTY MINUTES IS HOW LONG it took August to dress himself. To be more precise, twenty minutes is the amount of time he required to put on the shirt, slacks, socks, winter boots, and heavy Carhartt coat. Five minutes to button said shirt and slacks, zip up his fly, and tie the laces of his boots. The remaining ten minutes August spent observing himself in the mirror.

The clothing Reginald had chosen for him did not suit his tastes in the slightest. In less than an hour, he'd gone from looking like the disheveled, silk pajama-clad son of a distinguished businessman to someone who believed camouflage overalls was acceptable outerwear for any occasion. Not to mention the material was far heavier than what he deemed comfortable given his situation. At any rate, August exchanged his crutches for the lonely wheelchair sitting by the bedroom door. Its placement a conscious decision he'd made so as not to become entirely dependent on the damned thing.

The wheelchair itself was a gift from his father. Although the family business did not produce medical equipment, the Braeden Company did oversee the chair's fabrication and assembly. And with external consultants at his fingertips, August was given free rein to design a chair that would best fit his specific needs. To his father's disappointment, he had kept things rather simple. Aside from the wine-red padded upholstery (courtesy of Rolls Royce), the chair did not have many luxuries or automated components. When asked why he did not go with a motorized option, he simply shrugged his shoulders, which had further stoked the flames of his father's quiet anger. Truthfully, manually propelling himself from point A to B was one of the few ways he had to keep his strength up. Taking that from him wasn't an option.

August rolled out into the hallway. Hands rowed the wheels stolidly, eyes drawn to his left and right. He gazed upon the faces of Foxxes past and present. Men who contributed to their family's great legacy in one form or another. In his eyes, the portraits lining the walls captured dignity, strength, and resilience.

There was his father, Robert, of course, age forty-three, and the Braeden Company's current board chair. Then there was his grandfather, Alan, born in 1934, aged eighty-four and retired. His father before him, Marcus B. Foxx, born 1909 and died in 2015, was said to have been a hard-nosed and cruel man. When August met him, he had been a drooling human shell. A phantom fading in and out of existence. He would burst out in fits of perceived delirium, rattling off what sounded like gibberish.

"They're snakes. They're all snakes. I made a mistake. I trusted the snake. Forgive me." The man would plead, borderline scream the words, with his yellow eyes bulging in their sockets. How afraid August had been. Not due to the outburst itself but having believed himself to be looking at the future. His future. His mother said they'd never visit the care home again. She told Robert it was too much for August—for her. And they hadn't. The next and final time he saw his great grandfather, the man was in a box.

The youngest framed subject was Eric B. Foxx. Depicted wearing his military uniform, the man cut an imposing figure. His mustache and full beard made him look older than his eighteen years. Sadly, eighteen years is all he got. In the year 1918, he gave his life heroically while serving in World War I. His father, Thomas, who was born in 1880, had become stricken with grief. The loss of Eric had devastated him, and as a result, he drank himself to death. His liver quit on him in 1925. He was pictured with his twin brother Alexander, as it was said the two were inseparable.

Last but not least, for he was the beginning of it all, the architect; Braeden Foxx. There was no picture. No portrait. Fire had laid claim to those things long before August was a twinkle in his father's eye. A bronze placard immortalized the man's place on the wall. It read *Braeden Foxx, industrialist, philanthropist, pioneer 1850-1951.*

Where did August fit in among the greats? How could he

when he had been born wrong? He pondered as he rode the elevator to the first level of the two-story lodge. He tried to push the self-destructive thoughts out of his head. Tried to focus on meeting the manservant in the kitchen and uncovering his scheme. But they were loud.

"Ah, just in time," Reginald said.

"Am I?" August said, bringing his wheels to a halt just shy the kitchen island. The thing was massive. An antique that must've cost a very ancient tree its life. The black granite countertop gleamed.

"Indeed, you are." The manservant finished capping the lid on a metal thermos. He had spread a cloth across the counter to protect it. "How is the young master finding his accommodations?"

"Better than back home, that's for sure," August said, thinking about the yelling, fighting, and how he'd come to be banished. "I mean, I like the castle. But grandfather's lodge feels more like an actual home."

Reginald nodded. "Log homes tend to have that effect on people."

"So, I see," August said, then changed the subject. "What's all this then?" He gestured a hand at the spread cloth. On it, an assortment of unexpected things, ranging from a box of Jamison ammunition to a military-grade rucksack, seemingly stuffed to the brim with God knows what. Then there was the knife, looking like it'd come directly from the set of Rambo. But what stood out to him most was the freshly oiled 1876 Winchester rifle.

His father had never expressed any interest in guns, at least, as far August knew. He hadn't the time. The man was always on the move. He habitually hopped from one meeting to the next, abroad or otherwise, to oversee the Braeden Company's operations. His mother, on the other behalf, made her position on guns crystal clear. She detested them and banned all firearms from entering *her* house under any circumstance. His father did not object—meaning he did not care—so the rule went unchallenged. Therefore, the sight of the rifle lying on the counter was rather jarring.

"This?" Reginald said. He held up a steel thermos in each hand. "Why this is chicken noodle soup for you and tomato for me."

"That's not what I meant, and you know it." August narrowed his eyes. Leave it to Reginald to be sarcastic whenever possible. He pointed at the rifle.

"Right," Reginald said. He picked up the long gun. From it hung a well-maintained brown leather sling. "A gift from an old friend. An American. We spent many days in the Canadian wilderness stalking elk."

"Wait. You have friends?" August asked. He bit his tongue to suppress the urge to grin.

"Don't be cheeky. Of course, I've got friends. I wasn't always a butler, you know?"

"And you know how mother feels about guns in the house."

"No disrespect to the misses, young master, but it's just the two of us for the week, isn't it?" Reginald said. "Now c'mon. We've got somewhere to be." The manservant placed the remaining items in the rucksack, zipped it, and held it for August to take. "Think you can manage?"

August tested the bag's weight before accepting it on his

lap. "I can manage." The rucksack was deceptively light. "But you know how I feel about surprises. Besides, it's not even daybreak yet."

"Didn't know the young master was afraid of the dark." Reginald said.

"He isn't." August retorted. "See things from my perspective, will you?"

"I'm listening."

"How would you feel if you were the sole heir to a billion-dollar empire, forced to dress at such a god-awful hour, and rolled out into the dark abyss by your disgruntled butler? Whom, by the way, is totting a loaded rifle."

"Am I disgruntled?" Reginald stroked his chin coyly.

"You know what I mean." August said.

Reginald shrugged. "What can I say, Master August? This is the only retirement plan I've got."

"Har. Har." August rolled his eyes.

"Oh, come now. I thought that big brain of yours would have figured it out." Reginald said.

He wasn't wrong. August had an inkling of what was going on the second he saw the rifle but did not think such a thing possible for someone in his predicament. "From my understanding the sport of hunting requires a great deal of stealth. While I do appreciate the gesture, I'm afraid you're wasting—"

"I'm afraid *you're* wasting your time overthinking everything as you always do, sir." Reginald said abruptly. "This time I ask you to leave the thinking to me. Besides, without a fresh kill we won't have much of anything to eat around here.

A man should know how to live off the land regardless the size of his trust fund." He grinned.

"Is that your plan then, to make a man out of me?" August asked, musing over the situation. He was doing precisely as Reginald so boldly predicted by considering everything that could go wrong. How was he expected to navigate the woods? How could he blend in with nature? Wouldn't the tires of his chair hinder their progress through the snow? August did not want to be a burden. He knew the look when people had enough of his shortcomings. The way they attempted to mask their true feelings with sweet words of false reassurances. They would say things like *It's okay. Take your time. You got this.*

Reginald must have seen the gears turning in his head because his playful grin faded.

"You know, I was a bit younger than you when my father took me out for my first hunt." He said. "My younger brother made such a fuss about not wanting to kill. As for me? I was terrified of not being good enough for the old man. For good reason, mind you. He was tough. Cold from much of what I can remember. But on that day, not once did he raise his voice at us. He talked us through it, showed us what we needed to do. He taught us with a patience he'd never displayed before. So much so, I thought this man couldn't possibly be my father." August could see in the man's eyes he was reliving the moment. "I guess what I'm trying to say is this. He took us out knowing full-well we were inexperienced and didn't make us suffer for it."

CHAPTER 3

REGINALD COULDN'T HELP BUT WONDER if he'd overstepped back there. He hadn't intended to. But at his age, he knew how easily intentions could be misinterpreted. The boy's silence didn't help either. He hadn't said a word since they'd exited the house, but he had exited the house. That within itself was a good sign. Regardless, Reginald thought he should say something, anything to break the silence. He came up short.

Reginald Ristil was coming up on his 50th birthday. As a retired Gulf War veteran who served in the United Kingdom Special Forces, he hadn't pictured his life pivoting in the direction of form-fitting suits, polishing expensive cutlery, and child-rearing. In fact, after the war, he spent a great deal of his time in solitude, mostly tucked away in third-world countries where no one would think to look for him. A period of self-reflection of what it meant to be a human being.

Unlike many of his brothers in arms, he did not run to the church house for atonement. Didn't see any point in it. To utter a few sympathetic words and suddenly be absolved of all his wrongdoing? He highly doubted that was the way things worked in exchange for guaranteed safe passage into the hereafter. Instead, he focused on love. And what better way could he express love to his fellow man than to serve? To do so in earnest and without ego. Unfortunately, love didn't pay the bills.

When Reginald returned to the UK, he had taken on several jobs, with each one leading to the same end result. None of them were a proper nine-to-five, which meant he was paid under-the-table and worked almost exclusively at local ma and pa shops until they could no longer afford to keep him on. The last odd job he held was as a maintenance man at a rec center in Brixton. The place smelled like stale feet, but the prospect of room and board as a bonus was too good of an opportunity to pass up. He cleaned floors, toilets, wiped down equipment at end-of-day, and performed minor electrical work when needed. After hours he helped himself to the weights to stay fit. The gig lasted all of six months.

During Reginald's final week at the rec center, a physical altercation broke out between a group of boys amid a heated game of basketball. He did not know what the argument was about at the time, nor did he care. His concern had solely been on the knife a boy had produced. To argue and scrap was one thing, but to kill your fellow countryman over a petty disagreement was despicable in Reginald's eyes. Naturally, he intervened. An intervention that nearly cost him the inner peace he'd worked incredibly hard to forge for himself.

No, he did not fight the boys. He did, however, snatch the would-be stab victim out of harm's way with alarming strength. The act had turned the attention of everyone present onto him. It wasn't a good look. Especially when the boy he rescued had begun shouting to be released just as two officers came bursting through the doors. Reginald knew the owner, Pete, must've phoned them the moment all hell broke loose. Unfortunately for him, the cops arrived at the right place at the wrong time. The group of boys had come to focus their energy entirely on him. As for the boy whom he spared a trip to the morgue? He, too, turned on Reginald like a spouse who didn't want to see their abusive lover jailed.

Quickly and aggressively, the officers injected themselves into the mix. Thankfully Pete had been there to set the record straight. Better yet, Reginald recognized one of the officers who initially didn't know him from Adam on account of the beard he'd grown since they'd last seen each other. That time had been when they were in the military.

Lieutenant Crispin Barnett, now Officer Barnett, nearly shat himself when he realized who he was interrogating. Reginald vividly remembered their conversation from that day. After all, it was a conversation that forever changed his life.

"Jesus, Captain. What're you doin' in a place like this?" Barnett asked.

"Could ask you the same." Reginald said. He and Barnett relocated to a nearby watering hole to catch up. It was midday, so the number of souls occupying Gupt Sthaan were few but the spirits plenty.

"Fair enough," Barnett said. "Never had dreams of bein' a copper." He continued. "When I got back home, I didn't know what to do with myself. For months I'd just stay indoors and collect a check, ya know? Drown my sorrows and all that to avoid thinkin' about the things we did. The things we had to do."

Reginald nodded in agreement.

"So anyhow, one day I get a knock at the door. An old mate. A real blast from the past, ya know? He sees the state I'm in, invites himself into my home, and starts goin' on and on about the *good old days*. The whole time I'm standin' there thinkin' mate who gives a shit? We ain't kiddies no more. Then he asks me somethin'."

"What did he ask?" Reginald said patiently. Crispin always had a reputation for being long-winded.

"How'd you like to come back to the world?" For a long moment, Reginald and Barnett looked each other in the eye then roared laughing.

"For fucks sake." Reginald said.

"I said to him, are you bloody MI6 man? But he was serious." Crispin said. "He tells me he's a cop and that he could use a few good men to help keep Brixton in check."

"I can see your answer."

"Hold on. Let me finish."

Reginald repressed a sigh and sipped his beer.

"So anyway, I tell him I don't want to do no schoolin'. Then he tells me I don't have to. Says all I have to do is pass a physical, and I'm in." Barnett showed off his badge like a student whose teacher had given him a gold star.

"Good for you, Crispin," Reginald said sincerely.

"I can't complain. Brixton's not as bad as they made it out to be. Just people like anywhere else doing the best they can."

Reginald understood what he meant. They'd been to many places where people were doing the best they could and were doing it in tougher conditions than these. He had learned not to be so quick to make assumptions.

"Plus, there's little oversight. If there's a call, I go. If not, I'm here." Barnett said, gesturing to the pub's interior.

"Sounds like you've got it made," Reginald said.

Barnett shrugged.

"It was good seeing you, Lieutenant. If you'll excuse me, I need to get back to the rec and finish packing a few things."

"Captain. Wait." Barnett sputtered. "I didn't mean to pry back there, but I got to talkin' to Pete about you. I mean, before I knew you were you. He told me you just blew in like the wind one day askin' for work. I know you're tryin' to sort yourself out. I know I still am. What I'm sayin' is, I've got a bit of pull."

"No offense. But I don't want to be a copper. Had my fill of uniforms, thanks." Reginald said, standing.

"I didn't mean a cop," Barnett said cautiously. "Look, I do some security work now and again. Just to fill in the gaps, ya know? Make a little extra on the side. Last month I was part of a security detail contracted by a pretty high-profile client. You've heard the name Braeden Foxx, yeah?"

"Who hasn't? Nineteen-year-old genius who founded the Braeden Company back during the Industrial Revolution. Or so the school textbooks say."

"That's the one. You see, the family's lookin' for some live-in help. Not my type of gig. From what I hear, no one can seem to cut it. Robert, the man of the house, is a real knob. Experienced that for myself. His wife Veronica isn't much different, but at least you can talk to her. They've got a son that requires a lot of extra attention."

"The boy touched in the head or something?" Reginald asked.

"No, not at all. A cripple, actually." Barnett said. He took a napkin from the dispenser. When he tried to write on the napkin's blue surface with his ink pen, he cursed. The pen's blue ink blended in with the paper. He flipped the napkin over, found it scarlet on the other side, and tried again. "Like I said, most who go for the job don't last long. But for a guy like you? I think it'll be a cakewalk.

Reginald hesitated then accepted the napkin. He stared at the crimson paper and the bright blue inked numbers standing out against it.

"If you decide to give it a go, just call that number and tell them you got it from Crisp. They'll set you up for an interview."

"Thanks, Crispin."

"Oh, one more thing, Captain. If you make the call, do consider a shave."

CHAPTER 4

AUGUST HELD THE FLASHLIGHT WHILE Reginald pushed him in the wheelchair. The manservant had been right; it was cold. However, the snow he was worried about had already been cleared. Together they navigated along the path leading from the lodge to the edge of the woods. The lodge itself sat on one hundred acres, most of which were trees. The exceptions were the pond installed by his grandfather, who loved to fish, the horse stables, and the two-mile-long gated drive.

August thought about what Reginald had said to him in the kitchen. The man's words had been kind and encouraging. Closer to surrogate uncle than manservant. He thought he should say something, but what? He felt saying thanks would only understate his appreciation. On the other behalf, he did not want to go on babbling like a fool either. He opened his mouth to speak.

"Alright then. End of the line, young master." Reginald said, bringing the chair to a stop and locking the wheels.

Caught off guard by this, August blinked. He'd been so wrapped up in his thoughts he didn't realize they'd reached the tree line. "We're there already?"

"Right you are. Unfortunately for us, your chair can go no further. Fortunately, I can." Reginald said. He took the rucksack from August's lap and slung it on his shoulder opposite the rifle.

August watched with wide-eyed skepticism. "What exactly do you have in mind?" He asked, a cold spot developing where the rucksack had laid across his legs.

Reginald stooped, removing his feet from the chair's footrests. Repositioning the rifle from his shoulder to his hand, the man did the unexpected by giving August his back. "On you get."

"Excuse me?" August said, flabbergasted. Reginald couldn't be serious. August hadn't accepted a piggyback ride since age ten, and even then, he wasn't a fan. Under the guise of play, the method had been used to transport him from one location to next. He lost interest when he saw through the clever ruse and sought after his independence, to his parent's dismay, when it came to getting around.

"You heard me. On you get." Reginald repeated. "While I have the utmost confidence in your abilities, I won't have you wading through a foot of snow. Trust me when I say, there's a whole lot of nastiness beneath that white powder."

August considered for a long moment. "Alright," He said, swallowing his pride. "But this stays between us."

RUN RABBIT RUN

"Master August, if your parents knew what we were up to, I'd without a doubt be packing my bags."

August rolled his eyes. Reginald wasn't exaggerating, though. Once his father had walked in on the manservant demonstrating the proper way to perform a rear-naked choke. The man had shouted loud enough to raise the dead. If not for August insisting that he was okay and had every right to learn to defend himself, Reginald would have been terminated on the spot. And so, the lessons continued, with a few caveats, of course.

WITHIN TEN minutes, August grew comfortable in his new position secured to the manservant's wide back. He listened to the snow crunch beneath Reginald's boots and the song sung by the black-capped chickadees. In the distance he saw what looked to be the silhouette of a tower stretching to the sky.

By the time they reached their destination, twilight was upon them, and the flashlight was no longer needed. The tower in question turned out to be a deer blind, whiter than snow, and the first August ever laid eyes on in person. It looked strange framed by the bruised purple sky. A stark-white treehouse with spiraling weather-worn wood staircase leading upwards to a blackened doorway. Nothing at all like the ones he and his grandfather saw on the late-night cable access show Marksman of Beast. This blind was like something out of a fairytale, mysterious and enchanting.

"Doing alright back there?" Reginald said.

"You mean aside from not being able to feel my face? Peachy." August said. When they initially left the house, the temperature was indeed frigid, but now standing smackdab in the clearing, the atmosphere had become almost inviting. It was as if they'd stepped into a pocket of warmth despite the abundance of snow on the ground and lack of sunshine.

"Yeah, well, like a mate of mine used to say, suck it up buttercup," Reginald turned and, very carefully, lowered himself until August's rump came in contact with something flat and chair-like.

"You really did think of everything," August said. He withdrew his arms from around the manservant's neck. He hadn't noticed the utility vehicle until he was firmly planted on its bed. Like a malformed shadow, the UTV's dark green camouflage made it blend in with the lingering early morning shadows.

Reginald adjusted the rucksack and replaced the rifle on his shoulder. "You ever try toting a seventy-nine-kilo buck? I sure haven't. Don't want to either."

"Yet you somehow manage to tote that fathead of yours." August smirked.

"You know what? Keep being a smartass, and it's going to be you tied to that rack instead of the buck." Reginald said, clearly joking. All the same, he pointed out the power loader mounted on the UTV's front.

August threw up his hands in mock surrender.

"Alright then. I'm going to run our gear up, and then it'll be your turn. Try not to wander off." The manservant's words may have come across as cruel to the uninitiated. To August, his words were the equivalent of a store clerk offhandedly saying to a blind person, come back and see us again soon. He was unbothered. Besides, he did have a tendency to wander off. If not for his crutches being left back at the house, he would have made it his mission to explore. Without them, he was almost as useless as a beached whale.

Briefly, he watched the manservant ascend the spiral stairs. He thought, at any second, the rickety wood would give, and Reginald would fall victim to gravity. He was relieved when he disappeared out of sight and without incident. In times like this (times where August was left to his own devices, having little else to do), he resorted to what he did best.

Cushioned by the thick insulated jacket and wool cap, he laid himself back on the UTV's bed and stared up at the wintry sky. This far north away from city life, he could still see stars up there. The bruised purple hue was fading, becoming a more bluish grey. He thought about his parents. His mother, Veronica, was beautiful, tall, and fair-skinned with a lukewarm temperament. For all the fussing over him she did, the days she couldn't stand to be bothered were becoming increasingly obvious.

When he was younger, his mother smiled often, but these days she rarely smiled at all. Her beauty, too, was fading. He blamed her excessive day drinking for that and blamed his father for being the reason she drank at all.

Robert the Tyrant, an unflattering title whispered at family gatherings and professional functions alike to describe his father. Everyone knew what a monster the man was. Fortunately for them, they weren't trapped under the same roof with him for no more than a few hours at a time. Tall, thin, with wavy black hair, and piercing green eyes, Robert was what his mother described as complicated. August preferred the term mental.

His father always found a reason to stir shit up. He was clever at creating just the opening he needed to hurl insult upon insult at his wife. He would call her liar, deceiver, and creature with inferior genes. Held her liable for what he described as August's cursed nature.

August heard every word every time. Although he was never on the receiving end of his father's verbal assault, that didn't make him feel any less ashamed. Ashamed because he knew if he could hear the exchange, then so could Reginald. For that reason, he always felt like the biggest coward in the world.

But what could he do other than listen whenever his mother was forced to plead her case? He would writhe as she tried to convince the man she married that she was white. She had even offered to take a DNA test while sobbing uncontrollably.

Only recently did August muster the courage to intervene. Enough had been enough, and he could no longer sit idly by while his father treated his mother like complete and utter garbage. He recalled entering the master bedroom of their ancestral home and shouting at the top of his lungs demanding his father to stop. Two things happened. One, August had been unable to suppress the tears that rolled down his face as he shook with rage. Two, his father had done as he commanded.

He remembered his mother picking her naked self off the floor. She had used bed clothes to haphazardly cover herself. No, his father hadn't struck her. For whatever reason, he never resorted to physical abuse aside from maybe pushing. The madness behind his mother's nakedness was the man's way of humiliating her further by inspecting her skin for brown patches.

RUN RABBIT RUN

He recalled his father's cellphone ringing, which had broken the awkward tension in the room. Without saying a word to either of them, he had answered the call and left.

August dwelled on what happened after. Like a specter, his mother had drifted over to him, draped her arms around his neck, and laughed in a half-drunk, half nervous kind of way. Kings Cuvée had been on her breath. She cradled his face forcing their eyes to meet. The way she had looked at him was not the way any mother should ever look at their son, and he had been frightened. With her face pressed alongside his, she had whispered, "Oh, sweet rabbit. This is your fault. All of it."

In the near vicinity, a branch snapped, silencing the chickadees' song. August sat up, thinking it was Reginald descending the ladder, and quickly wiped away any stray tears to avoid interrogation. A deep snort stalled him and seemed directly responsible for the hot gust of wind against his face. His presumption was correct. Peeking through gloved fingers, he saw only darkness at first, but upon lowering his hands, his chest tightened.

Before him stood a living shadow. No, the creature was flesh and blood and hair. Hair so dark it devoured sunlight like a black hole. Never in his life had he seen, let alone heard of a black stag, yet here one was right in front of him. It was massive and could have weighed no less than one-hundred-and-eighty kilos. Its estimated height an intimidating two-point-four meters tall. If the stag got spooked, well, it would be game over.

"My God." August croaked in response to the stag closing the distance between them. His heart was jackhammering. The stag's ebon antlers formed a countless number of sharp points that shimmered like polished stone. He was beautiful.

Carefully August retreated backward into the UTV's bed until there was nowhere left to go. They were face to giant face. August turned his head away, shutting his eyes to avoid starting a staredown. He read somewhere on the Internet, looking a wild animal in the eye long enough was a surefire way to provoke it. He obviously didn't want those problems.

Again, the stag snorted. Its large snout nudged August's chest aggressively, and if not for the utility vehicle's metal frame at his back, he would have toppled over. That would have been better than being pinned as he was now. His breaths came in short rapid pants. He tried to scream but couldn't. His hands reluctantly went to the stag's face, pushed it, but the beast didn't give an inch. He was suffocating. Where was Reginald? How did he not know what was happening?

Then he heard it. Felt it. A voice inside his head that wasn't his own. "Look at me." The voice commanded.

August did not know if it was fear or astonishment that made him obey. He cracked open his eyes. For a second or two, his vision was blurry then cleared. The stag watched him with unmistakable intelligence in its large emerald eyes. Nestled in its huge blacker than black head made the glowing spheres appear to float. Captivated by them, he barely noticed the reward gifted to him. The stag had withdrawn its touch alleviating the pressure on his chest, allowing him to suck new air into his lungs.

He gasped but did not divert his gaze. He did, however, become lightheaded. The surrounding woods began to spin, ramping up faster and faster, swallowing up everything except the colors black and green swirling together. The stag's presence washed over him, invaded him, filled his mind completely like thick tar.

August outstretched his trembling fingers towards the beast. They breathed in unison. Radiating off the stag, he could feel power, wisdom, lust, and rage. When his fingers touched down onto the stag's coarse hair, the world ceased to be.

CHAPTER 5

AUGUST AWOKE TO DARKNESS. ON the wind, he smelled salt, tasted it on his tongue, felt it on his skin; dry and itchy. He was thirsty. The song of the black-capped chickadees had been replaced by crying gulls overhead. Barefoot, he could feel the ground beneath his feet. Not freezing snow, but cool sand between his toes. He noticed that he was standing. His legs were stronger than they'd ever been.

Unfamiliar voices chanted in perfect unison. The eerie harmony drilled him from the front, left, and right. "One eye on the stars. One eye on the veil. One eye on man. One eye on hell. One eye turned towards the heavens. The sixth will soon tell."

At his back, he could feel an intense heat and knew it to be fire. The disembodied voices continued to chant. "One eye on the stars. One eye on the veil. One eye on man. One eye on hell. One eye turned towards the heavens. The sixth will soon tell."

"We beseech thee." A singular woman's authoritarian voice rose above the rest. "Please hear our humble cry. Come forth through this living vessel that is Ninian. Ninian, king of the forest. Ninian who cures the sick and breathes life into the dead. Ninian who is opposite of you and answers his subjects not. He hears no one. Sees no one. Gallivants the lands selfishly. But you, the Pale, answers the cries of your children. Rewards us for our good deeds. For this we are eternally grateful. For this, it is us who will reward you tonight under the virgin moon."

August didn't know what the woman was on about. All he knew was no matter how hard he tried to fight against the binds around his wrists and ankles, his body wouldn't respond. It was like sleep paralysis. Except he seemed to be wide awake.

"A fearless boy." Another woman spoke. "His heart beats with a steady rhythm."

August felt knuckles brush the back of his head. Darkness gave way to light as the cloth covering his eyes fell away. He saw where he was. Or, more accurately, where he wasn't. Michigan had somehow become a distant memory. In its place a darkened beach where long shadows danced courtesy of a roaring bonfire.

"He comes from a brave lot." The authoritarian woman said. Her name Ánna.

Unable to turn his head to the left or right, August strained his eyes, but that didn't work either. Whoever these people were, they stood just beyond the reach of the bonfire's light.

He could see an arm here and a leg there, but their faces were masked in shadow.

"What's the meaning of this?" A man's voice boomed. August was startled as the man's voice seemed to have come from nowhere. The woman called Ánna stepped forth. He felt sudden heat rush into his face and reactively tried to divert his gaze. The fire's light revealed the woman's nakedness to him. Not that August had never seen a woman naked before. The Internet was full of naked women to ogle over whenever he got that particular itch all guys tended to scratch at one point or another. But for a woman to be standing right in front of him wearing nothing but her birthday suit was brand new. He felt both embarrassed and somehow ashamed.

Ánna was fair-skinned, muscular, her breasts firm and her nipples pink. Her hair was the color of wildfire, and her deep ocean green eyes glinted with a dangerous knowing. "You're a slippery one." She said.

"What's the meaning of this? Untie me at once." The man boomed again.

August's chest rumbled, and he understood. The voice hadn't come from nowhere. It had come from within him. Or so he thought. When his head moved for the first time, neck craning to look back over a shoulder, his understanding grew. It was not he who was bound to the sturdy wooden stake with fire roaring at his back. Not physically, at least. Somehow he had become an unwilling passenger within a complete stranger's body.

"Caitlin. Why are you doing this to me? I thought—" The man continued.

"Thought what?" Ánna interrupted. "That my sister had

fallen in love with you? That you were safe enough to climb out of whatever rock you were hiding under and into a warm bed to bury your bone?"

"I have no idea what you're talking about." The man said. "Caitlin, please. Have I been anything but kind to you? England has its fair share of thieves, murderers, and perverts. I am not one of them. I have shown myself to be a do-right man."

"Play the fool all you want." Ánna scoffed. "Makes no never mind to us."

Like a serpent, the woman Caitlin slithered into August's field of view. The way she moved befitted the illustrations marking her body. Depicted in white paint, twin snakes coiled around each leg, caressing her crotch and buttocks as they wound their way up her torso, forming a spiral around each breast with their mouths open wide and tongues flicking at coral nipples. In a hand, she held a long bone-handled knife.

"We want what's inside you. That's all." Caitlin said. "Once we have it, you needn't worry no longer. No more running. No more hiding. You can rest." There was genuine sincerity in her big green eyes. She and Ánna were practically twins.

"When Caitlin first told me about you, I didn't believe," Ánna said. "For years I've been looking for you. We've been looking for you. A second chance for us. We can free the Pale One from the Veil and merge man's world with His. For so long has the Age of Dark reigned. So few Nephilim and small gods left, reduced to fanciful tales and myths. But with your blood and the heart of the Lifegiver Ninian, we will usher in a new Age of Light. An age where man will see the true face of his god and the realm of man and magic will again be one and the same."

"One eye on the stars. One eye on the veil." A third woman, whose name they did not speak, began to chant.

The wind snarled. The sky pulsed subtly as the waxing crescent moon rolled over to a dark landscape ravaged by even darker ink-like splotches. Each time the sky pulsed a hot white luminescence rippled the atmosphere. Through the stranger's eyes, August saw something. It was like holding the negative from one of his grandfather's ancient polaroid's up to the light. Something aquatic (maybe a whale) swam across the sky blinking out the moon for a split second. Then it happened again, but this time there was no whale. This time there was something else. Something nightmarish that pressed against the sky's thinning pulsing and bulging membrane. A serpent's massive underbelly slithered like a winding river between worlds. August held his breath, unable to wrap his mind around the phenomenon.

"As above, so below." The bound man uttered. He straightened himself against the wooden post.

"Most religious folk think it just an analogy. But we the initiated know better, don't we?" Ánna said.

The bound man did not answer. Even as Caitlin pressed the knife against his chest, he said nothing. All the same, August felt the cool steel give rise to gooseflesh.

"It's time," Ánna announced. "Time to spill the blood of red and white."

August needn't guess to know what they intended to do to the man. But nothing could have prepared him for what was to come.

RUN RABBIT RUN

As IF on cue, Caitlin began placing sensual kisses along the bound man's neck and chest. Ánna crouched before him in the sand. She dug her fingernails into his hips and bit his stomach just above his crotch. The bound man did not respond, and she seemed displeased by this. Regardless, she wasn't detoured from taking his flaccid penis into her mouth.

August wanted to cry out. Not from pleasure, but the lack thereof. His internal wails were driven by the excruciating sensation of his flesh being split open by the knife. Never in his life had he experienced such raw agony.

Blood flowed freely from the fresh wound. Traveled down the bound man's chest and stomach, half disappearing within his dark pubic hair. His eyes lowered on Ánna. She doubled her efforts despite the vibrant crimson soiling her mouth and chin.

Caitlin was no different. She assaulted the bound man's chest wounds with her tongue while using the knife to create additional lacerations. They were like creatures of the night. Parasites, eagerly gorging themselves to sate their vampiric bloodlust.

Ánna expelled him from her throat, "Come now. No need to play hard to get. Caitlin said you were plenty lively in her bed. Then again, we can always count on men to be led by what's in their pants rather than what's on their shoulders."

"Just as I counted on you, witch, to lead with your feminine wiles." The bound man said evenly.

Ánna grinned. "Is that so?" The shadows dancing across her face made her look hideous and aged. In seconds she had gone from beauty to hag.

"Caitlin." The bound man said. His voice just above the fire's bestial roar.

Caitlin looked at him, her tongue in mid-lick against his bloody chest.

"I love you." He said. The words spoken with such conviction they seemed to compel the woman to cease her actions indefinitely.

Ánna laughed. "Delusional. Must be the blood loss. But stick with us. We've still got a ways to go."

Caitlin did not hear her sister. Holding the man's gaze, a thick fog dimmed the light in her eyes. Her demeanor transformed rapidly from vicious predator to docile lamb. She withdrew the knife from his chest and, in doing so, caused him to wince with discomfort for the first time. The ten-inch blade had been lodged roughly two inches in his right pectoral. "And I, you."

She reached down, nestled her fingers within Ánna's red curls. The touch must've come across as encouraging because the woman did not spare either of them a glance. That is until Caitlin yanked her head back so hard she yowled like a wildcat. The knife first slashed across her shoulder, then again along her neck, flesh giving way to steel.

Ánna screamed. She tried to scramble away, but Caitlin tackled her. Sand sprayed up in a plume, and the wind carried it in the right direction. She rubbed at her eyes in sheer desperation with one hand while the other tried and failed to shield herself from the slashes raining down on her.

"Sister, sto—" Ánna started to plead. Her plead became a high-pitched pain-induced squeal. "My eye! My eye! You stabbed me. You stabbed me in the eye. It's gone!"

RUN RABBIT RUN

The bound man looked on with indifference, and through his eyes, August witnessed the brutality unfold. He wished he could shut them or, at the very least, look away. This was sick. Madness. A terrible dream that couldn't possibly be real.

Ánna had given up on her eye. She held her mutilated hands in a guarded position out in front of her. Several of her fingers were severed. A meal the gulls will be thankful for come daylight. Caitlin clutched the knife double-fisted overhead then brought it down repeatedly and savagely until the flailing stopped.

"We've got a runner." The bound man said. The third woman who had stopped chanting a while ago had taken off running down the beach. Caitlin dislodged the blade from Ánna's chest and stood. Mechanically, she turned on her heels, pointed herself in the direction the witch had fled and took off after her at an alarming speed. Her feet pounded the sand carrying her away from the bonfire and the bound man. In her absence, the fire seemed to cackle like a living thing. Then, in less than a minute, a bloodcurdling scream rocked the surrounding pitch black.

"No!" The trinity's third whined. "Let go. Let go of me. Sister, please. You aren't you. This isn't you." She kicked, screamed, and tore at the hand fisted in her hair to no avail. She was drug before the bound man and held there. "Please. I'll disappear. You'll never see me again."

"Tried that." The bound man said disinterestedly.

Without being told, Caitlin hacked through her sister's Achilles tendon. She screamed again, but this time she had good reason to. Her screams eventually dissolved into sobs.

The sound was a broken spirit accepting its fate. She was left alone. Long enough for the man's bonds to be undone, anyway.

IF THE eyes are windows to the soul, then this man's eyes are windows fixed on one of the nine circles of hell. August felt like he was watching a snuff film. The type of fucked shit people went looking for on the dark web and regretted finding. Except he hadn't gone looking. He had been sitting in the UTV's bed listening to the birds sing, eagerly awaiting his butler to descend the hunting blind to take him up. What transpired was him crossing paths with a fairy tale creature, and like the reality behind most fairy tales, this one was grim.

When offered the knife, the bound man took it. The prey had become the predator. August felt no joy in the man as he drew the blade across the woman's throat. The one named Caitlin did nothing to intervene. Like a sentry, she just stood there.

"You should have let me be." The bound man said. He watched the sand drink the woman's lifeblood. Her mouth opening and closing like a fish washed ashore. He seized her by the hair, twisted the long locks around his fist, and pulled. She did not come easy but came, nonetheless.

The sand stripped the serpent paint from her breasts, midriff, and legs as he dragged her the short distance to where light and shadow converged. When he turned her loose, the resistance had already stopped. The exception was the weight that came with maneuvering the dead. He snapped his fingers, and Caitlin appeared. Together they rolled the third onto her back.

"Give me room." The bound man said. Caitlin obeyed. "Did you believe I came to you by chance?" He knelt beside the dead. "I would lie awake at night; haunted. I can still smell them. Human flesh roasting like pigs." His lips quivered as he plunged the knife into her stomach. Then, no differently than a fisherman would his catch, he gutted her straight up the middle. It was messy work. Nothing at all like a seasoned hunter who sought to preserve the meat. He removed the stomach, liver, and much of the intestines. The hot innards steamed in the cold night air.

When satisfied, the bound man staked the knife in the sand. His nakedness sheened in a thin membrane of sweat. He wiped his brow, smearing his forehead red. For a moment, he surveyed his work then buried an arm inside the cadaver up to the elbow. In short order, he found what he was looking for, gripped it tight, and pulled hard. So hard that when it came free, he fell over. He held his findings up to the light. It was the heart.

The bound man took up the knife. Rolling onto all fours, he began to crawl. The distance not far but exposure and dehydration drained his strength. He came upon a black mass spread out on the beach. Whatever it was appeared to be more shadow than earthly being. The creature consumed the bonfire's light like a bottomless pit. But its large red eye reflected well enough to distinguish head from tail.

"Nothing is sacred to them." He said with a heavy heart. "Sorry, friend. I had to wait until you reached the point of no return."

The creature snorted, its breathing labored.

"I know. I will not pretend to be inherently good, for no man is." He looked at the heart he held. "It seems the stars have aligned in my favor. Although I did not count on them going this far." He brought the heart to his lips and kissed it. Then, opening his mouth, he bit into the organ. Lukewarm blood exploded in his mouth. Its metallic taste rolled across his tongue.

He ate and he drank until there was nothing left.

"Great Ninian. Your enemy is my enemy. I eat of their flesh. I drink of their blood. Through the blood, I inherit their wisdom. Through the flesh, I inherit their traits. Through you, Ninian, I inherit eternity." A hand was laid on the mighty stag's flank. Its heartbeat faint. The bound man carefully positioned the blade over the dull thumping that swelled against his soiled palm. The fire crackled on, the gulls squawked right on, and waves thrashed the faces of rocks. "From this point forward, you and I are one."

With both hands on the knife, he drove the blade into the stag's heart. Ninian laid his head in the sand and expelled his last breath. The stag's black, coarse hair twisted and stretched forth. Out of the darkness grew vibrant green vines dense with bulbs. All at once they bloomed in an array of colors far too complex for the human mind to appreciate. The vines continued to expand. Out of Ninian's wound, too, they came, coiling around steel, bone, and flesh. They did not stop until man and beast were indistinguishable from the fascinating topiaries found in castle gardens.

CHAPTER 6

AUGUST WAS KNEELING. HIS FACE turned towards the sky. His eyes rolled white and mouth agape. His outstretched arms made it appear as if he were in a state of worship. Yet not a single word, let alone sound, exited his lips. He could hear waves crashing, smelled salt on the wind, and the warmth of enclosure surrounded him. But he could see nothing other than a faint light high overhead. It wasn't enough. He was starving like a plant that had fallen into a dark well with no hope of experiencing the glory of sunlight ever again.

Coming from the hazy light, he could hear indistinguishable voices clamoring. They spoke in whispers as if not wanting to be overheard. The whispers deteriorated into aggressive hissing that gnashed at him like teeth. The light overhead dimmed rapidly, and August felt like he was being squeezed. It was then, did his surroundings began to quake. A deep chill sucked the warmth from his bones, and the pitch-black fractured like sheets of ice. The fractures took on blinding light rays akin to a sinking ship taking on water. The light continued to expand until everything was awash.

"August." A voice called. His ears were ringing like chapel bells. "August!" The voice hardened as his world continued to shake. The penetrating light dissipated, and his eyes went in and out of focus. When the paralysis broke, he began to thrash violently and screamed. An intense pressure pinned his arms to his sides. "Stop it! Stop it, I say! Wake up. Wake up, August."

August went rigid. Within seconds Reginald's mahogany face came into focus. "Reggie."

"You're alright." The manservant said, stress visible on his face. "I told you to stay with the UTV. What're you doing out here? What were you thinking?"

"Out here?" August parroted in confusion. The pressure he felt on his shoulders had been Reginald's heavy hands shaking him. Even now they continued to hold him with a firm grip. He looked around seeing no signs of the UTV or hunting blind. Just untouched snow and barren trees far as the eye could see. Daybreak was upon them.

"Look at me," Reginald said. "Tell me your name."

"What?"

"Your name. What is your name?"

"August." He stammered. His lips cracked and dry.

"Last name?"

"Foxx." August stammered again, shivering.

Reginald manipulated his arms back within the coat's

heavy sleeves. August didn't recall taking it off. His hands, numb and whiter than they'd ever been, were stuffed into a pair of wool camouflage gloves.

"Do you know where we are?" Reginald questioned.

"In the woods," August said. He had caught on to why he was being interrogated. He didn't think he had hypothermia. Then again, most people who died of the condition never knew they had it.

"Where in the woods?"

"Michigan. We're in Michigan. I'm fine."

Reginald looked at him for a long moment, then fastened the cap down over his ward's head. "Let's get you out of this shit."

Too discombobulated to protest, August accepted his second piggyback ride of the day.

AUGUST DID NOT attempt to track how long it took them to make it back to the blind. Instead, he had focused on the warmth the manservant's back provided. According to Reginald, it had taken them less than five minutes, and that was good enough for him.

The hunting blind's interior was a comfortable twenty-five degrees Celsius. The temperature was maintained by a state-of-the-art battery-powered system controlled by a wall-mounted dial. August sat with his back to the wall. In his hands, he cradled a cup of cooling chicken noodle soup. In his mind, he was trying to process what had happened.

It happened again, he thought. Just as Dr. Adjei said it would. It wasn't the first time someone found him someplace where he had no recollection of how he came to be there. He had been hallucinating. A side effect of sleep deprivation and his deteriorating health. Like walking into a room and suddenly forgetting why you were there in the first place. Except, in August's case, his brain would step outside reality. Sometimes he would blank out completely. At other times he was transported to fantastical, and more often than not, horrifying places. Conjurings of his imagination. Or, as Dr. Adjei put it, the brain's way of coping with the pain.

"Penny for your thoughts?" Reginald asked. The manservant was lying on his stomach adjusting the Winchester's scope.

Do you think I'll die soon? August thought. He didn't dare speak the words aloud. He shrugged.

"Soon as you've warmed up, we'll head back," Reginald said. "What was I thinking? I shouldn't have brought you out here."

"I don't want to head back," August said. He tasted salt on his tongue and sipped his soup to chase it away. He remembered the beach, the gulls, the three beautiful women, and the savagery that ran the sand red. It had all felt so real.

"Well, that's too bad because we're going."

"No," August said. "I want to do what we came here for."

Reginald sighed. "Master August, I can't take that risk. I need to get you back inside so you can take your medicine."

"I don't want medicine." August snapped. "You brought me here knowing the risk. Or was what you said before we left a bunch of empty words?"

"I acknowledged you being an inexperienced hunter,"

Reginald said evenly. "I said nothing about jeopardizing your life."

"I know what you said. I also know what you meant." August said. "You've never pitied me before, Reggie. Don't start now. I'd rather die out here doing something that matters than sitting around in some big empty house."

Reginald regarded him for a long moment with his dark brown eyes, then said, "Finish your soup. We'll wait for a while and see what comes."

AUGUST FINISHED half his soup before arriving at the conclusion that he wasn't hungry. He had spaced again, but not in the bad way like before. He wondered if Reggie had eaten and decided not to ask. The last thing he needed right now was for his mental state to be brought into question again.

Coming back to the world, August discovered himself lying on a makeshift pallet. The likes of which the manservant constructed using a thick blanket from the rucksack. He was on his stomach, arms folded under his chin, and for the first time aware of the view before him. Beyond the unorthodox window that went from ceiling to floor stood tall trees to his left and right. Their pale white bark difficult to tell apart from the snow and ice clinging to them. Between the trees' wide gate stood an endless open field blanketed by virgin snow.

"Comfortable, Master August?" Reginald asked. He was right next to him, lying on nothing but hard floor as he gazed through the rifle's scope.

"Peachy." August said. He doubted the question had ever

been uttered to any real hunter. Unless perhaps they were dying of consumption, or their would-be prey had gotten the better of them. "It's kind of impossible not to be in this fancy electric heated tiny house of ours. A genuine pair of pioneers we are."

"Battery heated." Reginald corrected. "And what can I say? Modern times make for modern comforts. Like your grandfather says—"

August beat him to the punch. "Never apologize for the amenities afforded by hard work." Of course, he knew his grandfather's mantra. The man had only said it a thousand times at every company function to inspire employees to work their fingers to the bone for a chance at receiving generous pay bonuses. Doing his part by (reluctantly) being there, he had looked into many hopeful and desperate faces. They had been depressing.

"So, he does pay attention." Reginald said.

"*He* doesn't have much choice." August retorted. He then asked, "Does it usually take this long? In the show I watch with grandfather, the hunters bag a kill in like twenty minutes."

"That's called video editing and TV magic." The manservant said. "For guys like that, the game's already fixed. They shoot what they need to shoot, then spend the rest of the day in some cushy hotel. Besides, patience is the name of the game when it comes to a man feeding himself the traditional way."

August sighed. "Fine."

"We can always head back if you prefer."

August ignored the not-so-subtle hint. There was something else he wanted to discuss but wasn't sure how to broach the subject. He was surprised Reggie hadn't said a word about it. A little annoyed too. The way he pretended everything was kosher as if they were on holiday.

"How do you do it?" He asked.

"Do what?"

"Pretend everything's normal. Ignoring the screaming, the shouting, all the stuff my father says."

Reginald must have been weighing his words carefully because he did not answer right away. "It's not my place to interfere."

Coward, August thought. But he knew that wasn't fair nor true. He was mature enough to understand what would happen if Reginald overstepped. It would be goodbye and good riddance.

"As for the *stuff* your father says, I doubt he believes half the things that come out his mouth."

"Mother sure believes," August said. "It's made her old. His words, I mean. He beats her down with them."

Reginald was no longer looking through the scope. Saying nothing, he studied his ward's profile.

"What's worse is she blames me."

"Your mother doesn't blame you."

"Yes, she does. She said so herself. She looked me right in the eye and said everything's my fault."

"Master August people have a tendency to say things they don't mean when angry."

"She meant it. How many times have I stood idly by while father berated her? I swear, most days, I hate him. Then there are days I want to be like him, and I don't know which is worse."

"It's natural for a boy to want to impress his father." Reginald said after a long pause. "And I'll tell you something else."

"I'm listening."

"Lots of children go their whole lives seeking their parents' approval. Many never get it. By the time they come to terms with that fact, it's already too late."

"Thanks, Reggie. Uplifting advice." August grimaced.

"What I'm saying, Master August, is that it's up to you to decide the type of man you want to be."

"An alive one," August grinned.

Reginald narrowed his eyes unamused.

"What? If anyone gets to mock my mortality, it should be me." August said. His first impulse had been to tell Reginald he already knew these things. But in truth, the prospect of carving out his own path was so foreign a concept it scared him a bit. "Do you think they'll get a divorce? Why else would they ban me here?"

"I'm sure your parents just need some time to sort things out." Reginald said.

"Yeah, right," August said, unconvinced. His words followed by a pained grunt. His legs were beginning to cramp as lying in his current position for long stretches was impossible.

"Perhaps you should take a break. Here. Let me help you." Reginald offered.

"Don't. I'm fine." August lied. His eyes focused straight ahead. He didn't understand the creeping nervous energy he felt. It was like a giddy anxiousness churning in the pit of his stomach. He thought if he took his eyes off the snowy field even for a split second, this opportunity would forever evade him.

"You're not fine. You're in pain."

August could feel Reginald's disapproving scowl. He didn't budge. "I'm fine. Leave it." But the manservant was right. He wasn't fine. But that did not change the fact he hated being told what was good for him. Like most boys his age, he wanted to be strong. He wanted to talk to people without them stooping down to him with their forced, uncomfortable smiles and the tiny voices they used to address him. Most importantly, at the moment, he wanted this hunt. "Just a few more minutes. Please." The pain crept further up his legs and into his crotch. His elbows and shoulders, too, ached from supporting his bodyweight while lying there on the floor.

"Just a few more—" Reginald conceded, his words trailing off. "August, look."

They came one by one out from between the trees. They moved timidly, their white tails erect like nature's exclamation points, and their ears perked, listening for the slightest sound of a potential threat. From their black noses expelled white clouds into the cold morning air. August's opportunity had arrived.

"I see them," August said. His voice just above a whisper and his chest tight. He was afraid if he so much as breathed too loud, he'd scare them off despite the great distance between them. There were five in total. No, six. He hadn't seen him at first. He couldn't have due to the way its hide blended in with the bark of the trees. The tall, muscular buck that proudly held his head high displaying its magnificent crown. "Incredible."

"Yes, he is." Reginald loaded the Winchester with a single round and chambered it. "Do you remember what I told you?"

"That a man shouldn't take pleasure in killing. A man either kills to eat, or he kills to survive." August had asked if the two were the same. To his surprise, they weren't. Although people did eat to survive, they didn't always kill to eat. Reginald's definition of survival was a man given no option other than to take a life to preserve his own. Regardless, if said life was man or beast. He wasn't sure. He had never killed before. At least not anything considered significant in the eyes of man. Who hasn't stepped on the occasional ant or swatted the trespassing housefly? In life, that was a given. However, this was certainly not that.

"Very good," Reginald said.

August watched him make minor adjustments to the scope. The rifle itself was seated in what he learned to be called a shooting rest.

"He's about fifty yards out. I obviously can't take the shot for you. I will, however, set you up for success to the best of my ability. After that, it's left up to you."

August felt afraid. The fear had manifested so abruptly he became nauseous and nearly vomited on the spot. Thankfully, unlike his searing nerve pain, the impulse passed. He took a deep breath to steady himself then removed the wool gloves. His boney fingers trembled. With Reginald's assistance, they traded places, and it was he who was now master over the gun. There came no surge of power or bristling of the ego. He was keenly aware that in his hands he now held a tool capable of great destruction. If anything, his comprehension of this further stoked the flames of his nervous energy.

"Do you see him?"

August focused hard through the scope watching as the buck sniffed at a doe. He thought they must've been searching for food themselves. "Yes."

"An eighteen pointer. Some people believe eighteen is a lucky number. Do you remember where the heart is?"

"Yes." August was suddenly hot and drenched with sweat beneath the thick layers he wore. The wind coming in through the window was a godsend.

"Remember, squeeze the lever as tight as you can. When you're ready, cock the hammer, take aim, then—"

"Pull the trigger," August said, finishing the manservant's thought. Through the scope, he observed the buck lift its head once more. It appeared to be looking straight at him. A chill ran down his spine. The pain in his body had become so insurmountable he wanted to roll over onto his back and cry. His hands tingled with the familiar sensation only sleeping limbs could have, his pelvis tender, and his legs under the assault of phantom needles.

"Breathe." Reginald said.

August's heart was thumping like a jackrabbit. He breathed in through his nose and slowly exhaled out his mouth. His world grew smaller. Reginald was saying something, but white noise swallowed up his words. For a long moment, he and the buck stared at each other. When he blinked, it blinked. When he took a breath, it took a breath. August, with effort, cocked the rifle.

"Squeeze the lever tight as you can," Reginald said.

August did not hear him but did indeed squeeze the lever.

Unaware of the manservant's guiding hand, he aimed at the buck's shoulder where he knew the heart to be. He pulled the trigger.

Click! The round did not discharge.

"Shit!" August cursed. He hurriedly wiped away the sweat accumulating under his nose. Unbeknownst to him, his palm was left red with blood.

"Don't panic boy." An unrecognizable voice whispered into August's ear. It was inhuman yet somehow feminine. "You've got time." The voice encouraged. What sounded like stressed, dry twigs, being bent to their limit, groaned and crackled in his ear. "You've got all the time you need." Stiff elongated things curled against his shoulders like fingers. Whatever it was, he knew its face was alongside his. Its long stringy hair was rust-colored, but he dared not look. "Focus." It coaxed. "Focus... Pull the trigger!" The voice shrieked. The rifle boomed like rolling thunder across the sky. The black-capped chickadees took flight, and the deer fled through the trees. The buck was the exception. The beast dropped like a stone into the snow.

"Well done, Master August. Well done." Reginald said stroking him between the shoulders.

August was panting, shaking like a leaf, and his face wet with pain-induced tears. *Not again*, he thought. How could he have had another episode this soon? They were becoming more frequent. Had Reginald noticed? He stared through the window until his neck could no longer bear the weight of his head.

CHAPTER 7

IF SOMEONE WERE TO ASK Reginald if he were at all surprised by the way things turned out, him saying no would've been nothing short of a lie. He had no expectations for August to get a kill. Let alone for them to see deer at all. While he had suggested the pantry was short on food, he had done so knowing the city of Redbreast was about a forty-minute drive from the lodge. Reginald had only one objective. The objective was to rescue the boy from his pit of loneliness.

In his experience, it was both unnatural and damming to keep a boy of any age isolated from the world at large. He did understand August's parents' concerns. After all, they weren't an ordinary family who could leisurely venture out into the public eye for just cause. Not to mention Veronica's endless worrying and hypothetical *what-ifs* concerning her son's medical situation. Even so, these things did not deter Reginald from taking calculated risks. August's limited exposure to mass media outlets made it possible for them to occasionally visit a comic book shop or electronics store while traveling. Of course, in these instances, incognito mode had been in full effect.

The UTV carried them through the snow. It bobbed and dipped, jostling Reginald and his ward whenever they encountered uneven ground beneath the icy white. As predicted, the day was shaping up to be overcast. Meaning there was little chance the temperature would rise above negative six degrees Celsius. For Reginald, it meant recovering the kill as quickly as possible.

He looked over at August and saw the boy was very much awake and very much exhausted. The handkerchief he had given him, which had been white at first, was now soiled with dark red splotches. A hot bath and a fresh change of clothes were in order.

"Won't be long now." Reginald said.

"You say that as if I'm bored," August said.

"I think we pushed our luck enough for one day. Won't take but a jiffy to secure the buck, then we'll head in."

"Fine by me, so long as I get a picture first."

"A picture? Afraid I didn't bring a camera along."

"Don't worry. I have this thing called a smartphone. You might've heard of it."

Reginald knew what a smartphone was and remembered they came equipped with a built-in camera feature. Along with a bunch of other unnecessary bells and whistles. *Overpriced and overcomplicated paperweights*, he thought. "Yeah, yeah. I get it. I'm old. Just don't go posting it on the web. Last thing I need is to have my ass chewed."

"As if. I'll post it to Ping!. The pic is visible for twenty minutes, then it's gone forever."

"Uh-huh," Reginald said. Ping! was a popular mobile app developed by former sonar technician Margarete Greene intended to provide a haven for youngsters ages thirteen through seventeen. The reason Reginald knew about Ping! is because Ms. Greene, armed with the knowledge of August's passion for technology, reached out to the Foxxes with the bold idea to recruit the boy to be the face of the app's launch campaign. She had passionately expressed how she came across an interview published by Brightest Stars featuring August and thought he'd be a perfect fit.

The niche, web-based publication, was owned by British mogul Alan Cook. His teenage sons Callum and Kensington were the decision-makers. They regularly featured youngsters from well-to-do backgrounds with a vested interest in promoting S.T.E.M. programs to youths across all demographics. In actuality, most articles came across as gratuitous wank sessions that were closer to condescending than helpful. Those were August's words, not his. The boy wouldn't have interviewed at all if not for his father applying pressure on him.

To Ms. Greene's disappointment, her offer had been declined. Reginald witnessed the rare occasion where August and his parents agreed on something. Had the woman not been overzealous, she would have noticed photographs of

August on the web were as rare as Franklin D. Roosevelt being photographed from the waist down.

"Forever sounds too good to be true." Reginald brought the UTV to a stop. Climbing out, he sunk several inches into the snow. He looked around and saw bright red blood splatter, but no immediate signs indicating where the animal it belonged to had gone. The shot fired resulted in an instant kill. The ultimate beginner's luck, if there was such a thing. Together, he and August witnessed the buck not only go down but stay down. "What the shit?"

"Is something wrong?" August asked.

Reginald walked to the UTV's front. Just as he opened his mouth to respond, the ground beneath his feet gave way. He grunted. His left hand moved in a blur, clamping down on the motorized powerlift's steel frame. His fall speed was significantly reduced, sparing him a twisted ankle or worse, a broken leg. August's alarmed cry was lost on him as he stared down into the partially snow-covered trench. From a distance, the ground had looked level. Had he not stopped them where he did, they would have plummeted headfirst, sustaining who knows what injuries.

At the bottom of the icy trench, he spied what he was looking for. On its side and growing stiff, the buck gazed up at him with a lifeless brown eye. Reginald squinted. There was something else down there. Something that nearly blended in perfectly with the snow. A white glove.

"Reggie? Say something."

"I'm all right. Stay where you are." Reginald released his hold on the steel bar and allowed himself to slide down the trench wall. Once at the bottom, he dropped to his knees beside the glove and started to dig. The glove was attached to a hand and the hand attached to an arm. His heart rate increased as wartime images resurfaced in his mind. He saw the living, the dying, and the dead. The arm was attached to a body. He continued to unearth his find, rapidly scooping and tossing aside great handfuls of snow. When finished, his breathing was haggard and what he saw left him astonished.

Before him, a woman sprawled in white tactical gear. He leaned forward, not thinking he would find a pulse but decided to check for one anyway. He paused, noticing something strange. The woman's lips weren't the telltale discolored blue associated with hypothermia, let alone death. Her brown skin was glowing, radiating warmth.

Reginald's eyes fell from her face to the blue sapphire pendant around her neck. It appeared to pulse subtlety. He removed a glove and pressed his index and middle finger to her neck against the carotid artery. Not only did the woman have a pulse, but the amount of heat coming off her was impossible.

CHAPTER 8

IT WAS CLOSE TO MIDDAY when they made it back to the lodge. Reginald had hastily drawn him a hot bath. August could tell by how the manservant moved that he didn't want the stranger left unattended for longer than need be. But Reginald had slowed down when it came to assisting him to remove his clothing. Neither commented on his bruised arms, stomach, and legs. When it came to his underwear, he insisted he could handle that business on his own. Reginald had left without argument.

The entire time August spent immersed in the bath, he dwelled on the stranger they'd found in the ditch. He hadn't gotten a good look at the person but knew they were female and black. Aside from Reginald, he did not know many black people. He never thought about it really. His world was his world, and in it, they rarely cameoed.

Where had she come from? He wondered if she was a kidnap victim. One of the ones who fought back so hard the kidnapper decided she wasn't worth the trouble, so chose to kill her like in the movies. There was no shortage of missing person's reports in Michigan. Most notably, Detroit. A week ago the abduction of a high schooler made headlines. A star athlete who attended the Eleanor Walker Institute for Beautiful Minds.

August knew these things because he went searching for them on the Internet. As someone in his position, who often traveled, getting kidnapped and held for ransom, was a real-world fear of his.

"Did you phone the police?" He asked, sailing into the sitting room on four wheels. Hearing voices he hadn't detected prior to entering the room, he brought the wheelchair to a dead stop. He listened, noticing the door to the connecting study was ajar.

"He's had another episode," Reginald said. He sounded like a man on the verge of losing his temper. "Yes, I'm bloody sure. It would be best for you and the misses to get here soon as possible. He's *your* son, for crying out loud. What do you mean is there anything else? Well, as a matter of fact, there is. A peculiar situation has come up. Hello? Hello?"

"That went well," August said as Reginald emerged from the study.

"How much did you hear?" The look on the man's face suggested he hadn't expected him so soon.

"Enough."

"I have to keep your parents informed. You know that."

"I know. I don't get why you waste the time. On a good day, father only pretends to care. Didn't sound like a good day to me. If you wanted results, you should have called mother. Then again, she would've gone into hysterics."

"And it's for that reason I report directly to your father."

"And it's for that reason they won't come."

"Do you want them to?"

"No. No, I don't. Are the police on the way?"

"Not quite," Reginal said. He moved to the open fireplace where two chairs sat opposite each other, and between them, a sturdy armrest-high circular walnut table. On the table rested a teapot along with two cups on saucers.

"I don't understand." August said.

"Come. Have some tea while it's hot." Reginald moved a chair to accommodate his wheelchair then poured them each a cup.

August was about to decline the offer. He was more interested in getting to the bottom of why Reginald was evading his question. On his way to the fireplace, he changed his mind. He paused at the coffee table positioned in front of the large leather sofa. The table hosted a metal tray with various surgical utensils and bloody gauze. Next to it a bottle of isopropyl rubbing alcohol and hydrogen peroxide. Then he saw her. The woman who had been buried in snow was now buried beneath blankets. "Is she going to wake up?"

"I'm not sure."

"Then isn't that more reason to alert the authorities?"

"No. I want to know why she was on the property."

August detected an edge in the manservant's voice he hadn't heard before. For a while longer, he looked at the woman. The amber lights burning overhead made her pecan skin appear to shimmer. He went to the fire then and took the tea and saucer onto his lap.

"I found this on our sleeping beauty," Reginald said, his eyes not leaving their guest. He produced a SIG P226 and placed it beside the teapot. "I undressed her to check for wounds. She'd been stabbed twice."

"Christ." August's brows knitted at the pistol. If he recalled correctly, it was commonplace for Americans to carry guns. They could do so lawfully and took pride in the fact. But carrying a gun was one thing and for a stranger to have one on the property was an altogether different matter. After all, the lodge sat on one hundred acres of mostly wooded land, and the closest public road was only accessible via the two-mile drive, gated off by a tall wrought iron fence. "Maybe someone tried to kidnap her." But who brings a knife to a gunfight and wins?

"I'd like to believe that. If not for the way she'd been dressed, I would. Like a damned mercenary."

There was a long pause. The word mercenary struck a chord in August. A chord that reverberated up his tailbone all the way to the crown of his skull. He knew a little bit about men and women who sold their souls to the highest bidder. His friend had taught him well about mercenaries.

Philippe Barzaga had been on holiday in Europe with his parents. He and August had met in-between interviews at Brightest Stars and quickly became friends. His mother, Eva Barzaga, was a Colombian American celebrity journalist who built her career on exposing companies for exploiting child labor and using shell entities to commit tax evasion. August's grandfather called the woman a tough cookie, and in the same breath, a nosey bitch.

Eva's latest claim to fame was a story that, on the surface, sounded closer to conspiracy theory than it did anything rooted in reality. Like those Creepypasta stories floating around on the Internet about lizard people and human organ trafficking, her claims seemed to fit right in. The difference between those stories and the one Eva had written was that she had concrete evidence to back up her words. Plus, she had a voice and millions of ears willing to listen. That made her dangerous.

In Europe, a child goes missing every sixty seconds. Philippe Barzaga, despite his mother's security team, was no exception to the rule. As in nature, it's ill-advised to corner a scared animal. You might get bitten, and Eva got bit hard. The animal she cornered was Hall & Freight, an international shipping company that delivers by land, air, and sea.

An anonymous whistleblower put the company on her radar. Apparently, Hall & Freight were shipping more than just scented candles and the latest smart technology devices. Organs, for example. Human organs that hadn't come from any hospital and delivered directly to the front doors of men and women with very deep pockets. The further Eva investigated, the deeper the rabbit hole went. She unearthed names that made her blood run cold. Prominent people she either knew or had interviewed at one point in time. She had no clue she'd been sitting right across from devils.

The day Eva brought the first draft of her story to her editor-in-chief was the same day the threats began. The usual bullshit she'd endured in past investigations; intimidating phone calls where someone on the other end of the receiver would say, *you drop this thing, or we'll drop you.* Eva did not drop it, and as a result of her decision, her son Philippe got snatched. The FBI was brought in. Along with Eva and her husband, they waited for a ransom phone call that never came.

The western world hadn't seen anything so heinous, or at least not on such a grand scale. Every major news media outlet's streaming service was hijacked by hackers who broadcasted fifteen minutes of their brutality before information security experts could disrupt the stream. Philippe had sobbed, screamed, desperately switched between speaking English and Spanish as he pleaded for his life. They had cut small pieces off of him at first. Then bigger pieces. The message was clear. *Don't fuck with the powers that be.*

After that, no media outlet in their right mind would publish Eva Barzaga's story. Her research burned to the ground along with her Beverly Hills home. She and her husband had been inside at the time. No one on the outside knew why any of it really happened. The media pointed the blame at the Columbian cartel. Eva emigrated from Columbia at age twelve, so the story was easy for the ignorant masses to swallow. A typical rags-to-riches tale of a little brown girl who emigrated to the US in the pursuit of the American dream. Too bad the little brown girl grew up to be a woman who couldn't escape her family's ties to the cartel. Edit. Save. Submit. To add insult to injury, a week after Eva's death, a video began circulating online of the deceased journalist being ravished simultaneously by multiple men whose faces weren't visible.

What was perfectly visible in the video was Eva Barzaga's wedding ring.

August never laid eyes on either video. One, because he didn't have the stomach for it. Two, because the Barzaga's had been his friends. For a long while he avoided Ping! and social media altogether. He knew the truth. He'd read Mrs. Barzaga's unpublished book with his own two eyes. Philippe had made that possible when he helped him gain remote access to his mother's laptop. All he had to do was visit the specified web address and August had taken it from there. He downloaded everything from Mrs. Barzaga's laptop over a VPN connection to a private server then offloaded the data onto an encrypted USB thumb drive. He kept the drive hidden in the chassis of an older gaming PC he and Reginald built years ago. If the stranger were a mercenary, then she'd likely been sent by someone who knows what he has.

"What are you suggesting?" August asked. He was uncertain if mentioning the USB would be a good idea or if doing so would only serve to feed the manservant's contagious paranoia.

"I'm sorry. I don't mean to upset you, Master August. But my question is this. Who had she been fighting with, and where are they now?"

August took a breath and put on his big boy thinking cap. They'd found the woman on the property approximately a mile and a half from the public access road. The road itself was marked by two bright yellow signs reading DEAD END in reflective lettering. A necessary deterrent for the naturally inquisitive. There were no businesses or other houses in the area, so the likeliness of someone turning on to the road by mistake was next to nil. On the other behalf, the lodge did sit empty for long spans at a time. It wasn't entirely illogical to suggest that maybe someone had cased the place, thought the property vacant, and decided to use the grounds as their dumping site for unfortunate souls. "I get it. You don't want to call the police because you mean to interrogate her, right?"

"Yes," Reginald said admittedly.

August gripped the blanket covering his legs a bit tighter. He thought about the USB drive again. Should he tell him? What if he was wrong? Or worse, what if the woman overheard him and managed to pass the information along to an interested party? He felt foolish. He was being paranoid. Maybe Reginald was, too. A mercenary? Really? His last name was Foxx, but his first name sure as shit wasn't Alan or Robert. His grandfather and father were the stars of the show. They were the ones who oversaw the Braeden Company's operations, which was the second largest privately held corporation in the world. Unlike Philippe's parents, his own had done a bang-up job at keeping the paparazzi at bay. Even though it had cost him some freedoms, never once had August experienced a sense of dread when it came to his safety.

Reginald must have seen the unease in his eyes because he next asked, "Do you trust me?"

August nodded.

"I cleaned and bandaged her wounds. I give you my word that she is at no risk of infection or death."

August nodded again.

"But we cannot turn her over to the authorities just yet.

Not until she's woken up, and I've had the opportunity to question her."

"But she's the victim, isn't she? We aren't above the law, Reggie. We can't hold people against their will."

"Master August, your safety is my number one priority. I know you're a good boy with good intentions, but you don't know the world like I do. Situations aren't always what they seem to be."

August knew that. But there was a distinct difference between being cautious and being cruel. "And I know if I woke up in a strange place after being stabbed and left for dead, I'd be terrified. Find her some clean clothes. If you must ask your questions, then she can at least listen to them comfortably."

CHAPTER 9

REGINALD RISTIL CHECKED THE TIME on his mobile then flipped it shut, returning it to the inner breast pocket of his vest. Like the sand in an hourglass, the day was steadily sifting away. He thought about all the things he should be doing, such as preparing lunch or checking to see if anything could be salvaged from the morning's kill. He highly doubted. The well-being of the stranger had taken precedence over the possibility of procuring succulent cuts of venison.

He had planned to spend the better part of the afternoon teaching August how to dress out a deer. Once done, he would have gotten them cleaned up, served lunch, and then retired to the kitchen to listen to some Zeppelin while planning the week's menu. But here he was reluctantly on the second level of the two-story home, briskly making his way back to the elevator. Draped over his left arm, a black Lululemon matching athletic top and bottom he'd found in the guest suite. In his right hand, a pair of Adidas running shoes.

It had crossed his mind to override the boy's authority on morality for the sake of keeping them all in the same room under his watchful gaze. The thought, however, had been fleeting. Reginald knew if the woman came to in his absence and attempted any fast movements, the stitches he made would be ripped open. He thought about the teardrop blue sapphire pendant the stranger wore around her neck. More specifically, the way it had appeared to glow when he found her and had done so without sunlight. Maybe his mind had been playing tricks on him because the pendant hadn't repeated its self-illumination since being indoors.

What really troubled Reginald was the stranger's unorthodox tattoo he'd discovered after removing her top. A fierce blackbird took up her entire midriff. Upon closer inspection, he'd seen the tattoo was composed of many perfectly segmented, smaller blackbirds that made the piece whole. He had seen enough ink in his day to know it was tribal. But what tribe specifically, he did not know. Many of today's remaining gangs identified as tribes. They had swapped out their flamboyantly colored, and more often than not, too-big clothing for less conspicuous garb. While using phrases and identifiable tattoos was nothing new, they had taken a front seat to the way they did things. However, the idea of a gang making an attack on the Foxx clan was laughable. They were neither sophisticated nor stupid enough to try.

Reginald paused in the hallway when the lights overhead flickered. What followed was immediate and total darkness.

RUN RABBIT RUN

AUGUST'S MUSCLES WERE at ease from the bath he'd taken earlier. This, in combination with the hot tea in his belly and the crackling fireplace, was a recipe for drowsiness. He intently watched the woman lying beneath the blankets in her unconscious state, or at least as intently as his heavy eyelids would allow. His eyes shut, then opened, shut, then opened. Like a skittish pup in a potentially hostile environment, he fought the sandman's lullaby. Reginald warned him to stay vigilant. To call him at once if their houseguest began to stir to life. He would have rather been up in his room exploring the countless simulators VRChat had to offer. Or anything, really, to curve his growing paranoia. Alas, he was playing sentry while the manservant was off doing what he asked.

In a well-practiced motion, August wheeled away from the fireplace. He repositioned himself at the end of the coffee table to get a closer look at the woman Reginald had sarcastically referred to as Sleeping Beauty. He surveyed the features of her face. She possessed high cheekbones, firm skin, and a smooth complexion except for the scar above her left eye. Her expression solemn, which all things considered, was to be expected. Nevertheless, she was, without a doubt, a beauty.

What captured August's attention most was her hair. It was shoulder-length, black as a raven's feathers, and twisted like thick tree roots. He imagined if she were standing, they'd hang like the vines of a willow. He thought about touching them, then looked down at his lap. One hand rested on his mobile and the other on the pistol Reginald had taken off the stranger.

It was well understood by the manservant that he did not have the compacity to kill a person, let alone shoot them.

Reginald promised that he wouldn't have to. He had told August that the pistol was in his care only as a precaution if the woman were to wake and go into hysterics. Because, in Reginald's own words, sometimes the sight of a perceived immediate threat had a way of sobering a person right up. If it came to that, he hoped he was right.

For now, August mustered the courage to satiate his curiosity. He bent forward at the waist, gingerly outstretching a hand to touch one of the stranger's rope-like locks of hair. He never got the chance. The hanging lights overhead dimmed, flickered, then went out. He jerked back his hand, startled, then sighed at his ridiculousness.

"What am I doing?" He muttered. He was unbothered by the sudden absence of light, and unlike many, did not have an irrational fear of the dark. Besides, the log in the fire was still burning. Not the most potent light source, but plenty for August to make out his immediate surroundings in the vast room.

He picked up his mobile to call Reginald, figuring the old house must have blown a fuse. He frowned. Pressing the smartphone's power button did nothing. He tried fingerprint recognition, but the outcome was the same. Impossible. The phone's battery life hadn't been close to dead. He held the power button and waited for the Android screen to appear. Nothing happened as he stared at his pale reflection in the black mirror.

"Hello?" A distorted voice crooned like an icy draft through the lodge.

August stiffened. The lodge boasted three main points of

entry; the front door, the attached garage, and the kitchen, all equipped with sensors to notify occupants whenever a particular point of entry was accessed. With the fuse blown, there had been no such announcement. Judging by how close the voice was to the sitting room, he determined its owner had entered the lodge using the front door.

The manservant's words before about wanting to know who left the stranger for dead had come back to spook August. He sat motionless, chest tight, ears listening.

"Why are all the lights out?" The voice demanded, growing closer and more refined. He did not hear footfalls cross the hardwood flooring. One moment there had just been himself, the stranger, and now there was a third. He felt breathing on the nape of his neck, slow and even. "Why are you sitting in the dark, little rabbit?"

"Mother?" He asked. The familiar citrus notes of Kings Cuvée tickled his nostrils.

"Who else would I be?"

"I thought you and father weren't coming."

"We were already in town. Your father was just being dramatic."

"But the two of you aren't due for a few more days."

"Did you really think we'd miss your birthday? Don't be a silly rabbit."

August cringed. He hated that fucking nickname. No matter how many times he told his mother this, she ignored him. She was drunk too. No surprise there. Perhaps even a good thing she was. The drink almost always dimmed his mother's perception, made her slow to fuss over him, but occasionally made her cruel. "Wouldn't be the first time." Nor the second.

"The last." She promised.

"Where's father?" August set his hand to a wheel to face her. His other slid the thing she hated most from his lap down to his side where the fire's light didn't reach. Never mind the unconscious stranger. If his mother laid eyes on the pistol, he would never hear the end of it.

"In the car." She said. "He's waiting for us." Her hands firmly gripped the wheelchair's handles preventing August from turning about.

"Outside? Isn't he coming in?"

"No, sweet rabbit. We must be going."

"We can't leave. There's a stranger unconscious on the couch."

"I see her." His mother said. She curled her fingers around his shoulders to comfort him. They creaked and popped like a bundle of dry twigs, the sound familiar and unsettling. Her weight shifted at his back, leaning down and forward until their faces were side by side. "I'm sure the butler will take care of it."

August's heart thumped. Was it happening again? Was he losing touch with reality? He had taken his medicine. He knew Reggie had put the tablet in his teacup the way he always did, and the hot tea dissolved it. He could still taste the bitterness on his tongue. In his peripheral, he saw nothing other than a curtain of black curls shrouding his mother's face. "Then I should put a jacket on."

"There's no need. It's not far from here to the car."

RUN RABBIT RUN

August swallowed. There was a nagging sensation scratching at the back of his mind, tapping away like Morse code. He turned his head slowly, daringly, to look at the woman he called mother and was confronted by tired green eyes. Freckles formed a bridge across her nose, spanning from cheek to cheek. She usually hid them with makeup. A process that never failed to make them late no matter how much time she was given in advance to be ready.

She was smiling her trademark lopsided tipsy smile. The fire's undulating light pried back Chronos's fingers, softening the lines on her face. August relaxed. She stood upright, took the chair by the handles again, and whirled him around. The speed at which she turned almost made him drop the pistol. Perhaps he should have but the scratching, tapping nagging, faint as it was, remained.

August and his mother hadn't gotten far at all when at their back, he heard what sounded like wings fluttering. Not small wings either but something far larger in scale. Wind whooshed, sending the fireplace into a frenzy and transforming shadows into long, menacing abstract shapes that streaked the walls and stretched to the high ceiling. The gust was so powerful it coned around his mother's torso ruffling his hair with violent fury. In alarm, he craned his neck to see the happening, but before he could, the room was blanketed in complete and total darkness.

He felt a tug at his hand that held the pistol and knew it was no longer there. As if oblivious to all of it, his mother's stride didn't break. His mouth opened dumbly. No words came out. There was only silence. Oh, so brief silence. Then the room

71

exploded in an orange fireball, and the smell of gunpowder singed his nostrils. The thunderous bang disoriented August as if Zeus himself hurled a lightning bolt inside the sitting room. His head buzzed with a thousand hornets, nearly missing the heavy thud impacting the floor. His chair crept forward a few more feet, then stopped.

Blankets that once billowed like the sails of a ship dropped to the floor, returning the light the fireplace provided. Everything had happened fast, ending as quickly as it began. August was frozen. All the color had drained out of his face, and fear rattled his bones. He wanted to turn around but couldn't bring himself to do it as death's presence seemed to loom over him.

Before long, the decision was made for him. *Sleeping Beauty* was wide awake and standing right in front of August. She was stark naked, her breast heaving, and sweat beaded her forehead. He saw, too, deep crimson was seeping through her bandages. Regardless, the eyes bearing down on him held no friendliness. She was gripping the SIG Sauer tight. Her finger on the trigger.

CHAPTER 10

"WHITE NOISE, DO YOU COPY? Operation Control Burn is in full effect. I repeat, Operation Control Burn is in full effect." The voice in his ear brought him back to the world. A world where the weightlessness he'd experienced in the void of time and space no longer applied, and again the face of his father had become a distant memory. His shoulder throbbed painfully, burned, from where the bullet had kissed his flesh in passing. However, it was Firefly's controlled but premature detonation that had nearly sent him on a permanent trip to the great beyond.

It took a second for his surroundings to come into focus behind the tactical gas mask's black lenses and a second more for him to get his bearings. The room he occupied glimmered unnaturally, and fire dripped like water from the ceiling above.

Reinitiating night vision, he saw the wall he used for cover had been reduced to a pile of flaming rubble. Ironically, the adjacent doorframe leading into the hallway remained fully intact. Through it, he could see black smoke rolling along the ceiling with the enthusiasm of a locomotive's smokestack.

"Go for White Noise." He said, standing to his feet.

"Captain. We thought you were dead." Firefly said.

"Not quite. A bit early for fireworks. What's happening?"

"Yeah, about that. Sorry. The order to detonate came straight from the Source. We tried reaching you on coms. Must be some interference in the area."

"Firefly. Sitrep. Now." White Noise interrupted. The surrounding fire was spreading fast.

"Right." Firefly said. "Bloody Yanks pushed up our timetable. At zero-three-hundred, Baghdad is going to become one gigantic fireball."

Operation Control Burn was said to be a contingency plan, but White Noise had known better than to believe that. In actuality, it would've been initiated regardless of the outcome of his team's mission.

Months prior to the mission, Firefly, their demolitions expert, arrived at Baghdad's prestigious Al-'Adudi Hospital. With the assistance of a few opportunistic insiders, the man set explosive charges in place without raising suspicion. White Noise understood his team, The Huntsmen, were expendable. He understood too that even in the event of mission success, the charges would be blown, reducing the ancient hospital to dust. America's bombs would unknowingly aid in covering up their dirty little secret.

RUN RABBIT RUN

The mission was simple. Eliminate the traitor Roderick Ellis and punish Baghdad for harboring him. The inevitable outcome underscored the chilling significance of The Huntsmen insignia located on his right shoulder armor plate. The insignia depicted the Greek goddess Adrestia as a winged skeleton. In her left hand, she held an empty hourglass, and in her right, she wielded a sword. Outlining the insignia in Greek, read the words *she cannot be escaped*. And no one escapes the queen's retribution.

The Huntsmen were the human component; the eyes that could see and the mouths that could bring peace of mind where big explosions at times left room for doubts. All they need do was pull a trigger and utter the words *threat neutralized*.

"Understood." White Noise said. "What's my extraction point?"

"The courtyard's out unless you're feeling bulletproof. Baghdadi ground forces and Fire & Rescue are moving on the building as we speak. The new rendezvous point is the southside rooftop. You've got ten minutes. By the way, were you able to lay eyes on target?"

White Noise scanned the room. He spotted the remains of one of the guards charged with protecting Roderick Ellis. The guard had managed to get a shot off on him before taking two rounds in the chest in rapid succession. After, he had trained his weapon on Ellis and pulled the trigger a third time. The man had been looking straight at him, lying on his sickbed, and his face a flushed matrix of veins. The round had entered Ellis's right temple and obliterated the back of his skull upon its exit. Then the explosion had happened. "Threat neutralized. I'm in route."

He observed the dead man's half-charred remains. He knew then that this would be his final assignment. He was neither young nor as dumb as he used to be. He no longer had a taste for death and carnage. He'd seen the world one-hundred times over, stuck his cock in every color of the rainbow, and his anger was all but depleted. Most importantly, he'd gotten shot this morning. Not that he hasn't been shot in the past because he had. What made this occasion different was that it could have been avoided. He was slowing down, and to be slow, made him a liability. It was best to go out on top. It was best not to jeopardize Queen and Country.

"Copy that." Firefly said.

White Noise felt the temperature rising and knew the flames were gobbling up every ounce of available oxygen. Just below his right hip, he wore two miniature canisters. Each canister held a four-minute supply of oxygen. He turned the release valve on one, delivering a steady stream of clean air to the breathing apparatus attached to his gas mask. Next, he raised his rifle, carefully slicing the pie, as he first cleared one corner and then the other before stepping foot out into the empty hallway.

Al-`Adudi was aesthetically closer to palace than hospital. Over the years, it had undergone several renovations where modern amenities were carefully interwoven within its interior while preserving the original architecture and decor as much as possible. For this reason, the majority of the art lining the walls were original pieces, some dating as far back as the thirteenth century.

White Noise moved at a brisk pace down the seemingly

never-ending corridor, passing several darkened doorways in his wake. He did not have the luxury of time to check each one for a possible ambush. Besides, he didn't need to. He was confident that he was the only one on the floor armed with a deadly weapon, and the Baghdadi ground forces below would have to go through a baptism of fire to reach him, courtesy of Firefly. His biggest threats currently were smoke inhalation and the rapid spread of flames that roared with the ferocity of a pursuing dragon.

While someone uninitiated might have given in to the temptation to sprint or run, White Noise knew to do so would be fatal. The faster he moved, the harder his lungs would need to work. The harder his lungs worked, the quicker he'd deplete his oxygen canisters. He also had to consider the additional thirty-six kilograms of gear he carried on his person. All in all, at the pace he was moving, he was making good time.

The stairs were coming up on his right but what he hadn't counted on was for the structural integrity of one of the corridor's high archways to fail. He was forced to clumsily redirect his steps to avoid being crushed by gigantic falling stone and consequently fell hard against the wall to his immediate right. The floor trembled and quaked beneath his boots as the punishment of the falling rubble continued a mere few feet ahead.

Embers stirred in the chaos of dust and debris, and White Noise's eyes, upon lifting them, were inexplicably drawn to the painting hanging on the opposing wall. The oil in the paint gleamed from perspiration, shimmered in a way that drew the eye to its center. The piece depicted a large thirty-six-point buck reared on its hind legs. Before it, a medieval Islamic maiden dressed in traditional garb mirroring present-day appeared to dance with the deer.

The pair were encircled by women who looked on with expectant expressions. Their eyes twinkled with mischief framed between their hijabs and niqabs. In the painting's background sat a stone altar offering grapes, corn, wheat, and honeysuckle. Meanwhile, in the twilight sky, a new moon was in the process of being born.

The longer he stared at the painting, the more real it became. He could smell the grass as it was torn up by the buck's hooves, watched it shake its mighty antlers gallantly, could hear music in the form of vocals harmonizing. His equilibrium waned as he watched the women bow and sway, linking their hands together, revolving clockwise around the buck and maiden. Stopping, then going again, but this time counterclockwise, gradually increasing the pace faster and faster, round and round.

White Noise's head spun like an out-of-control carousel. What he was seeing became a blur of images, a flipbook where each image complimented the next, creating a fluid, constantly changing animation reel. But these images weren't cartoons. They were flesh and blood. In one instance, the maiden and the buck danced merrily. In another, the maiden was stark-naked, bountiful black curls sweeping her shoulders, and her olive skin sheened with sweat in the cresting pale moonlight. All the same, they danced.

The surrounding women no longer linked hands but now held knives that seemingly manifested out of thin air; their bleached white handles fashioned from bone. Again the reel changed. The maiden threw back her head in ecstasy as she lay on the altar, crushing grapes and corn kernels under her back. Her legs held firm around the buck as it ravaged her savagely. She also had a knife. In the throes of the buck's climax, the maiden slit its throat open in a curtain of blood, and the surrounding women rejoiced in loud zaghrouta.

The reel changed for a final time. In the grass lay the buck's carcass, and the maiden straddled him, excavating the creature's steaming heart. She bit into its flesh, chewed, and swallowed, then stood to her feet, raising the large organ overhead in triumph. The women exploded in another celebratory cry. Their many hands outstretched, caressing and stroking the maiden's blood-soiled belly. The newborn moon was a deep crimson and appeared to have torn open the sky during its birth. It was at that moment did the maiden's green-eyed gaze meet White Noise's.

"Are you death?" The voice asked in Arabic. White Noise understood the words, but he did not comprehend the question. The words were sudden in his ear, breaking through whatever hold the painting had on him. On impulse, he turned on his heels to face its source, raised his weapon chest level, and fired off a single round before sighting the threat.

There occupying the doorway of a patient room, stood a child, a boy significantly shorter than himself. The kid couldn't have been no older than eight and wore a hospital gown. The empty shell casing clattered to the floor and rolled away. White Noise's breaths were labored, borderline hyperventilating beneath the gas mask he wore. He was drenched in cold sweat and his heart pounding so hard his ears throbbed. What had he almost done?

"Are you death?" The boy asked a second time, his voice trembling. White Noise watched him teeter forward then back, forward then back, in a disoriented sickly fashion. The night vision made the boy look ghoulish. More so was the case when blood trickled down his forehead and rolled off his nose in continuous drips. He saw then the destruction left by the single round he had fired.

Where there should have been hair and flesh and skull, there was nothing. The top of the boy's head was gone. What remained was a deep dark trench of brain matter and skull fragments. The boy teetered forward once more, collapsed to his knees, and crumpled against the doorframe.

In Hollywood cinema, writers write about mercenaries, assassins, and military combatants, binding them to two main rules of engagement. The rules being that they could kill neither women nor children. Reality was more complicated, and White Noise had seen his share of child soldiers armed with automatic rifles and grenade-wielding women with hate-filled eyes. Why then did he feel the acidic taste of bile rising in his throat?

He dry heaved, tearing his eyes away from what he had done. That painting. What was that sick shit? And those haunting green eyes that seemed not to look at him but through him, to his soul. He hadn't felt fear like that since first enlisting. He had been exposed under her gaze. All the things he'd done and would do laid bare. Was *he* death? The question lingered while his eyes fell back on the destroyed thing that, not even two minutes ago, had been a living, breathing child.

RUN RABBIT RUN

He looked at the lifeless sack of flesh and bones and thought, *what was one more body in a city that was about to become Armageddon?*

Yes, he was death's avatar, and he had done his job. He had to go. He had to get to the extraction point.

White Noise lucked out. Although it nearly crushed him, the fallen rubble didn't hinder his path. He laid a booted foot hard into the door leading to the stairs. It gave, striking the wall with so great a force, the glass pane embedded in the door shattered. In the stairwell, the floor was hot beneath his feet, and looking over the railing, he saw fire raging. At least he did not have to go through hell to get to heaven.

He ascended the steps swiftly to make up for lost time and simultaneously opened the valve of the secondary oxygen canister. But just as quickly as his ascension began, White Noise was forestalled by a powerful vice clamping down on his ankle from behind. The paralyzing pain stopped him in his tracks. He whipped around, finger on the trigger, but this time he did not squeeze. He did not squeeze the trigger until he dropped his gaze, and his eyes beheld the impossible.

It crawled towards him on its belly. Gnarled fingers consisting of exposed yellow bone and seared flesh dragged it up the steps. A man on fire, yet he did not scream his agony. Maybe he couldn't scream. Maybe the same heat that was cooking his flesh had already disintegrated his lungs. But if true, why wasn't the burning man showing any signs of slowing down? Why was White Noise unable to break away from the fingers coiled around his ankle? A grip that intensified the more he struggled.

He made the decision then. Fired a single round into the poor bastard's head to put him out of his misery. He fired another round into the burning man's back for good measure. The man lay still.

"Why are you here?" Demanded a voice emanating from the burning corpse. White Noise was taken aback. He must've been losing his fucking mind. There was no way in hell the man could still be alive. First, the green-eyed woman with her penetrating gaze, then the child he murdered—whom he'd likely done a favor anyway, or so he told himself to justify his mistake. Now, this thing was staring at him, crawling towards him again with its grip renewed. Its face a patchwork of olive skin and raw pink flesh void of lips, and its eye sockets blazed brightly with the intensity of a furnace.

"This is madness!" White Noise yelped, switching his firearm from single-shot to full-auto. Shots rang out in rapid succession, bullets punching hole after hole into the reanimated cadaver, and the empty shell casings sang like small chimes as they impacted the floor.

Click! Click! Click! He had emptied the entire magazine. The burning man kept coming, dug its fingers into his clothes, and climbed his person until they were face to grisly face.

"Why are you here?" The burning man snarled. White Noise could feel heat wafting against his face and smelled brimstone on its breath. "Why are you here black man? This is not your war."

White Noise went for the bowie knife on his utility belt, but before he could unsheathe it, a sharp pain spread throughout his left side. He snarled, staggering against the wall at his back, and for a split second, his vision doubled.

RUN RABBIT RUN

The surrounding stairwell flickered like an old television set. When the flickering stopped, his brain was convinced that it occupied two places at once. Yes, he was in the stairwell, but he could also see the transparent overlay of a rustic ritzy hallway lined with portraits of men wearing stern expressions.

He drew back his head then slammed his forehead into the burning man's nose in a spray of blood and fire. The stairwell started to fade, and the lodge's rustic hallway began to solidify. Again, in desperation, he headbutted the creature with all his might tasting blood in his mouth. It was worth it because this time, the stairwell was altogether gone. He could see the knife digging into his side and knew well the portraits on the wall. He was not White Noise. That call sign had died well over a decade ago. His name was Reginald Ristil.

"August." He croaked, fighting for supremacy over the knife. While Baghdad had not been real this wretched creature was. He needed to get to his ward. He needed to not die.

CHAPTER 11

"You killed her. You killed my mother." August said. He could hear himself again over the fading hornets buzzing around in his hand. The words fell from his lips in a hoarse, barely audible whisper. He was shaking with fright and his arms becoming fatigued in their half-raised state. Fear told him it was necessary to keep them up best he could. Told him not to make any sudden movements so as not to provoke the inevitable any quicker than need be. His mind agreed, and the body was willing but unable to comply for much longer, and in the end, fatigue won out. His arms shakily touched down on the chair's armrests. "Why did you do it? You didn't have to kill her."

There were days when August did not like his mother but never were there days when he did not love her. That love evident in his glossy eyes. But it wasn't sorrow that caused them to brim with tears. Hard as he tried, there was no sorrow in his heart at all. His emotional response was catapulted solely by fear. A selfish desire to live, to not meet the same fate as his mother, to not be executed like some mad dog, or more accurately, the helpless rabbit she viewed him as.

Reggie had openly expressed his suspicions about the woman being a mercenary. August had been positive the man was being paranoid. To say the least, the thunderclap of the pistol made him a believer. His thoughts ran wild, thinking about Eva Barzaga, Philippe, and the USB thumb drive. He stared past the barrel of the gun aimed at him, and although the woman was fully nude, displaying everything a boy his age would be interested in seeing, August stayed her gaze.

"That thing was not your mother." The stranger said. Her voice was firm and unapologetic. She winced, lowering the pistol and pressing a palm flat to her bandaged side.

"What did you just say?" August stammered in disbelief. His fear transformed into anger and confusion. Anger because he thought he had known better than Reginald and was proven wrong in the worst way possible. And confusion because the woman was obviously delusional. A real psychopath.

"Look at it. See for yourself." The stranger stepped aside, no longer blocking the light emanating from the fireplace.

"I won't." August shook his head. No, he did not want to see that. He did not want to see what remained of his mother. He refused, feeling the lump in his throat thicken and the knot in his stomach tighten.

His reluctance must have provoked the stranger because

she was stalking towards him, the distance between them closing rapidly, and the pendant around her neck bouncing with a faint glow.

August reared back, but she was behind him in a flash, preventing him from retreating further. He felt her fingers around his neck, strong and callused. "Stop it. Let go of me."

"Look. Open your eyes and see."

"I said let go!" His fingers tore at the stranger's hand in desperation. Her other hand wrapped around his jaw, angling his head towards the floor. August could feel the pain he experienced during the morning's hunt resurfacing in his joints. "Reggie. Where are you?"

"We don't have time for this. Open your eyes, boy. You need to open your eyes and see the truth." The stranger said evenly. A peculiar warmth radiated from her very being. August's grip on her wrist loosened and the muscles in his shoulder fell slack.

August's eyes slowly opened.

"Take your hands off him." Reginald's booming voice filled the room. The manservant stood at the landing of the stairs clutching his gut and looking worse for wear. The distance between him and the stranger might as well have been miles apart because he wasn't faster than a speeding bullet, nor was he bulletproof. He did not appear to be armed either. Well, unless the bundle of clothing tucked under his arm could be counted as a deadly weapon.

"Stay where you are, butler. He must see." The stranger said, standing upright.

Reginald took a determined step towards them. In

response, the stranger raised the pistol and took aim, stopping the manservant cold. He appeared to be weighing the situation.

August kept his eyes to the floor, hearing them but not really. It took a bit for his eyes to adjust, but they did. His heart rate quickened in anticipation. To him, the floor looked otherworldly, a purgatory place teetering between dark and light. He was reminded of the cheesy late-night televangelist who came on during the nights after he and his grandfather finished watching Marksman of the Beast.

The slick-talking preacher man with his slick preacher suit had once said, "the light has a way of revealing gruesome truths." August felt that way now, knowing a gruesome truth was lying on the floor at his feet.

"I promise this won't end well for you." Reginald said.

The stranger made no response.

August saw what was on the floor in glimpses. A bare shoulder partially covered by black straw-like hair to an arm visible from the elbow down. He did not realize he had started to breathe through his mouth, having a borderline panic attack. Still, he leaned forward in his chair for a closer look. He saw the bottom half of her face and how the jaw was twisted and the mouth frozen in a state of eternal anguish.

"Reggie. You need to see this." He said, unaware that he was whispering. The teeth were wrong; brittle, crooked, and discolored.

Saying nothing, the stranger gestured for the manservant to come forth and stepped aside, keeping a measured distance between them.

Reginald hesitated but came. He grunted as he stooped

down beside August, producing his lighter without being told. A single flick hardened his face into a tight grimace.

"Now do you see? That thing is not your mother." The stranger said. No, it most certainly was not. Light has a way of revealing gruesome truths, and again Reginald flicked the lighter.

August stared in bewilderment, breathing through his mouth right on. The thing, this twisted horror lying on the floor, looked like it climbed straight out of a piece painted by Zdzisław Beksiński: a blasphemous merger of humanity and mother nature. But there was no flesh to speak of no more than there was blood from the gunshot wound that had destroyed its head. No flesh. No blood. No bone.

"This isn't possible," August said. He knew what his eyes had seen; his mother's freckled face, her listless green eyes, the beginnings of crow's feet from crying entirely too much, and that hopeful little smirk of a smile. What he saw now was not his deceased mother, yet the revelation brought him no relief, and the knot in his stomach tightened. This unfamiliar thing. This mangled humanoid husk. This inanimate creature with ashen skin that wasn't skin and deep narrow vermillion trenches carved into flesh that wasn't flesh. Its very existence defied logic. Yet here it was, and it had almost whisked August away to God knows where if not for the stranger's intervention. "It was my mother. It was her. I swear."

"No, Master August. It was not her." Reginald said reassuringly.

"Then what is it?" August asked.

The manservant cautiously dipped his fingers into the

substance spilling from the twisted thing's head. He brought them to his nose and sniffed. "Soil. Black soil." He said, then turned his eyes to the stranger. "Planning on just standing there? Or are you going to tell us just what in the hell is going on here?"

The stranger watched them coolly. "Those clothes… are they for me?"

CHAPTER 12

August listened anxiously to the words the stranger spoke. He, Reggie, and the strange woman had been talking for a while, so long that dusk was upon them, making the power outage all the more apparent.

Truthfully, he and Reggie sat there doing their best to make sense of what was said. Most, if not all of it, sounded like complete and utter rubbish. But seeing was believing.

"That thing. What did you call it?" August interrupted.

The three had gathered by the great stone fireplace. August and the stranger sat opposite each other, separated by the repositioned coffee table. Reggie was standing. The manservant twisted, snapped, and broke apart the twisted horror. Tossing its bits into the fire, they squealed and crackled like dry kindling.

"A birch golem." The stranger said. She was redressing her wounds and showed no visible discomfort as she did. "Golems are complicated and powerful magic. People who wield this type of magic are dangerous. Strong."

August noted her accent. The likes of which he surmised originated from the African continent. From which country exactly, he did not know.

"Excuse me. Did you say magic?" Reginald said, his skepticism obvious. He dusted off his hands and buttoned his bloody shirt to hide his bandaged gut. Sweat glittered on his face and forehead. Knotting the blue tie around his neck, he pulled it snug.

"Yes. I know this is difficult for the two of you to process, but what I say is truth." The stranger said.

"No, I don't think you do understand," Reginald said. "Master August was nearly taken by that *thing*, for whatever reason, and you'd sit there and tell me magic is to blame for its existence? Bullshit. Maybe it's a rare subspecies yet to be discovered. But magic? Oh, come off it."

"A rare subspecies of what? Walking trees?" The stranger fired back, fury igniting in her eyes.

August took the opportunity to look at her. Really look at her. She was older than him but much younger than Reggie: perhaps mid to late twenties. The way she sat with her back straight and head held high reminded him of the majority of his mother's friends and their soon-to-be debutante daughters. But unlike them, she was visibly athletic, and because of the type of clothes given to the woman, there was no hiding her muscularity.

If he had to compare the stranger to someone, it would be American boxer Claressa Shields, who he came across some time ago while binging boxing highlights on the Web. His gaze dropped to her midriff, scrutinized the tattoo there best he could but had difficulty making it out against the stranger's dark skin. A kind of bird, August was sure of that much.

"How the hell should I know? I'm not a biologist." Reginald strained to keep his composure. "What I do know is that none of this madness was going on until you arrived."

"If not for me being here, the boy would already be dead." The stranger said evenly.

"If not for you being here, I would've never let Master August out of my sight."

"Stop it. Both of you." August interjected. It wasn't lost on him the way the two sized each other up. He couldn't blame Reggie for his apprehension. He felt the same. After all, the stranger was the one with the gun. Although she showed no signs of aggression, he felt no less a hostage in his own home.

He hadn't expected his words to get through, but they had. His heart galloped, feeling their eyes watching him. "I didn't mean to shout." August cleared his throat, forcing his eyes to meet theirs. "But bickering like this will get us nowhere. You said time isn't on our side, right?"

The stranger nodded.

"Okay then. You're right. We don't understand any of this. To be honest, everything you're telling us sounds downright mental. But I can't deny what I saw. Neither can you, Reggie."

The manservant crossed his arms.

"Try seeing things from our perspective. Reggie's number

one priority is my wellbeing, but you're the only one sitting here with a gun. And for all the talking we've done, we still don't even know your name."

"My name is Seko." The woman said after a long pause. She removed the SIG's magazine, unchambered the remaining round, and placed the weapon in the center of the table. Keeping the magazine, she slid the bullet inside. "Veil-touched are what we call people born to the world with gifts you think of as magic. Imagine them like satellite dishes pointed to the sky and picking up signals broadcast way from outer space."

"You mean, like another dimension?" August asked.

"Yes, exactly. For some veil-touched, the signal is very weak. Never realized in their lifetime. But for the rare few, the signal can be immense. That is what we are dealing with here."

"These *veil-touched*, why do they want Master August?" Reginald said with lingering reservations.

"I am not certain." Seko said.

"I'm afraid that's not good enough, Ms. Seko," Reginald said. "Tell us, how exactly do you fit into all this?"

"Like you, it is also my duty to protect the boy."

"Is that so?"

"It is. I take it you both have seen my tattoo?" Seko used the index fingers and thumbs of either hand to frame the fierce avian inked on her midriff. She turned towards the fireplace, and the black ink shimmered and stood out against its pecan tan canvas.

Not having seen many tattoos up close, August, was taken aback by the level of detail. He could make out each individual feather in the bird's spread wings, its beak sleek like oil, and the smaller birds that made the piece whole. He thought it must have hurt a lot.

"This is how Magpie marks all its little birds." Seko said.

"Magpie?" August raised a brow.

"For centuries, our organization has protected prominent individuals threatened by forces deemed supernatural."

"I've never heard of no such organization." Reginald said.

"Nor should you have. Servants come and go without ever knowing we exist. This is not to be taken as an insult but a good thing. When we have to make ourselves known, the circumstances are rarely pleasant." Seko said.

"Are you saying my parents hired you?" August asked.

"No, not exactly. In our experience, the affluent are the most likely to come into possession of a powerful artifact. Most have no clue what they have. Then there are those who do know, which is always worse. Not to mention the ones whose long deceased relative made a pact with a malevolent entity or devil. One day out of the blue, the entity comes to collect the debt."

"This is lunacy." Reginald blurted. "Ancient artifacts and demonic contracts. What's next? Little gray men skulking about with probes?"

"What happened to your stomach?" Seko's question struck like a blunt instrument.

August wanted to know too.

Reginald's eyes hardened. He hesitated then said, "I was making my way back downstairs when the lights went. Damn near gutted myself on the railing. Now it's my turn to ask a question. In the snow… what happened to you?"

Seko eyed the manservant for a short while. "A day before you were to arrive, Magpie sent me as a precaution. They were right to do so because something was here waiting for you."

"Something like what?" Reginald said.

"A golem. One more advance than that one there." Seko cast her gaze to the fire as it consumed the creature's charred remains without complaint.

"How do you mean?" August asked, his eyes followed her gaze. He shuddered. He was glad Reggie had broken apart the twisted thing and fed it to the fire.

"No one golem is the same. They are created. Designed with a unique purpose in mind. The golem I encountered, I think, was meant for you." Seko looked at Reginald.

"And what makes you say that?" The manservant asked.

"Like I mentioned before, the veil is not accessible to everyone. It takes a great deal of energy to construct a golem, let alone one proficient in complex tasks such as hand-to-hand combat and the use of weapons. Are you not ex-military?"

August was surprised by the question, while Reginald did not react at all. He knew the man had served in the military but never once had it come up in conversation. He figured it best not to ask, so had scoured the Web for whatever information he could find. To his dismay, the manservant hadn't been some special forces operative, but a military cook held in high regard.

"When we found you there were no signs of anyone or anything else. You were alone." Reginald said.

"Then that means *we* are not alone." Seko said, her voice grave. "Two golems. One destroyed and one severely damaged and no indication of who its master might be."

Reginald nodded, stroking his chin. He opened his mouth to say something then appeared to change his mind.

"None at all?" August frowned. "Forgive me, but I don't believe you're telling us everything. You said so yourself that you were sent here as a precaution. In my experience, precautions are based on evidence that a potential threat exists." His life was full of potential threats, according to medical professionals. Climbing stairs, bathing, and walking were just a few of the hazards plaguing his daily life. Mediocre tasks that he was privileged to watch people take for granted day in and day out.

But life wasn't so bad, really. On the contrary, it was his parents who made certain aspects of his existence unbearable. The constant arguing, the nagging over his well-being, and his father's negligence whenever they occupied the same room. All times where his differences were most highlighted.

"Three," Reginald said. He sounded like a man lost in fog.

"Three what?" August said, exasperated. He was at his wits end with Reggie's snark remarks.

"Three golems." Reginald bent forward and rolled up his right pant leg. He drew from his sock a knife as long as August's forearm and a hundred times sharper than his boney elbows. He placed it on the table. The blade pointed at Seko.

"Is that meant for me?" She asked.

"It was meant for me," Reginald said. "I got lucky. One of those things attacked me while I was on the second floor. Stuck me like a pig. That's what happened. I wanted to say something before, but I thought I was losing my damned mind."

"Is it dead?" August inquired. His eyes bright with fear and uncertainty. He thought about those zombie movies where one of the unsuspecting protagonists kills a zombie, leaves the area, only to return later to discover the body is no longer there. The last thing they hear are those moaning groans breathing down their neck and shuffling feet.

"Yes."

"Are you sure?"

"I'm sure," Reginald said patiently. "And for the record, I agree with Master August. You aren't telling us everything. The way I see it, we need to put all our cards on the table."

Seko did not seem to be paying them any mind. She was studying the knife. She turned it over in her hands, seeming especially fixated on the handle's craftsmanship. "Take a look at this." She leaned over the table and presented the knife to August. "Careful. The blade is very sharp."

Heavy too, August thought. He noticed this immediately upon accepting the knife across his palms. He knew little about knives except for their usefulness when it came time to do the eating thing. He gave it a once over. The blade itself was pretty ordinary despite its length. As for the handle? It was undeniably the centerpiece.

Bleached bone white, the handle was elegant, like something preserved that whispered heirloom and old world. He imagined someone had carved it by hand ages ago because the attention to detail was incredible. He rotated the knife. On one side was the face of a beautiful woman with big eyes and long flowing hair with no end in sight. The other side depicted a buck from its head down to its chest. It wore an impressive rack of antlers, and between them floated a crown that looked to be maybe vines or perhaps thorns.

"I'm not sure what I'm looking at here." August admitted.

"A knife used in rituals," Seko said. "The sacrificial kind."

"I'm guessing the kind that doesn't involve a goat," Reginald commented.

"Me? They want to kill me? But why?" August's voice went up an octave, and he fumbled the knife in his hands. Reginald caught it before he could hurt himself. In doing so, August glimpsed the knife's flat butt. There he saw a perfect symmetrical moon with tiny notches for craters. He thought about the nighttime beach, the angry pregnant sky, the blood.

"That's not going to happen." The manservant said.

Seko shook her head. "To answer your first question, Magpie is always on the lookout for irregular otherworldly activity. We are the little blackbirds that line the wires of telephone poles and land on your windowsill day or night. It is through their eyes that we know when veil forces with malevolent intent are at work. Someone or something has set its eyes on you, boy."

"My name isn't boy. Stop calling me boy." August bristled. He didn't particularly care what she called him. What bothered him was everything coming out of her mouth introduced a new and more terrifying revelation. She had been spying on him. Spying! On him! What had she seen? Oh god, he hoped she hadn't seen him doing *that*. Anything but *that*. The thought alone turned his ears red.

"August." Seko sighed. "We need to know who or what we are dealing with. But I need your help."

"How?"

"Tell me. What do you dream when you sleep?"

August was further unnerved by the question. Up until

recently, his dreams were what was to be expected for someone his age. The usual incoherent nonsense where one minute he would be engrossed in a fantastical world standing alongside elf-like creatures battling against hordes of the undead, and in the next, he was free-falling only to awake mere seconds before impacting the ground.

Then there were those new intimate dreams. The ones that had become more frequent, taking precedence over elves, legions of undead, and goblins. They were replaced by his high school crush Gloria Chambers.

The girl was an outsider much like himself, ridiculed for attending the private school on academic scholarship. She was called *charity girl* to her face and behind her back. August did not see her scholarship as something she should be ashamed of, though. If anything, unlike most of the students whose mommies and daddies paid their way, Gloria had earned her attendance.

Not only that, but August thought she was pretty with her curly chestnut brown hair and hazel brown eyes. It had taken him what felt like an eternity to earn her trust. Which at the start of their awkward friendship manifested in the form of a kind smile.

He did not blame her for distrusting him at the start. She had been, after all, a lamb thrown into a den of lions. Sure, August looked harmless enough in his wheelchair, but even a maimed lion still had teeth. In the beginning, he imagined whenever Gloria looked at him: she saw a big sign that read APPROACH WITH CAUTION. If at all. So he had taken it upon himself to approach her.

N. A. WILLIAMS

Of course, he had first psyched himself up. Social status aside, August was not immune to butterflies of the stomach or his breath hitching in his throat whenever their eyes met. So yes, the sudden invasion of these strange dreams about Gloria Chambers meant waking up many mornings, frustrated and embarrassed, but neither of which was the reason behind why Seko's question unsettled him.

"I don't dream," August confessed. "Most nights, I don't even sleep."

"Don't sleep?" Seko parroted.

"Chronic insomnia." Reginald put in.

"For how long?" Seko said.

August's shoulders rose then fell. "About a month, I'd say." It felt longer.

"But before, you did dream, yes?"

"If you can call it that. It never felt like dreaming to me."

"Then what did it feel like?"

"I'm not sure. It's hard to explain. At night I would shut my eyes and the whole world shrinks away. There's only darkness. Darkness and—"

"And?"

August fell silent, his eyes downcast. He could see his great grandfather Marcus's sagging face and bulging yellow eyes. He could hear the old man raving, muttering disjointed phrases, pleading forgiveness for an ambiguous crime. The adults had ignored him because they were accustomed to it. August could not. He had stared, dreading and wondering if crazy ran in the family. He wondered if crazy was running through him now, eroding reality and therefore eroding his mind.

"Darkness and what?" Seko's patience sounded strained.

August lifted his eyes to her, hesitated. "Darkness and voices whispering. When I open my eyes again, it's morning."

"Voices?" Reginald questioned, and August felt judgment pressing down on him. "These voices, what do they say to you?"

"I don't remember."

"August," Seko said. Again, she leaned across the table. She closed a hand over one of his and gave a gentle, reassuring squeeze. Her touch was like fine sandpaper. However, unlike his, her hand was warm, borderline hot. "I once heard someone say cold hands make for a warm heart." It was as if she read his mind. "Think, August. Try to remember."

"I told you already. I don't remember." He did recall the darkness and the sleep paralysis. Each morning left August feeling like a piece of himself had been chipped away. Instead of waking flustered and feeling guilty with lingering thoughts of Gloria Chambers on his mind, he awoke exhausted more than he had been the night before.

When his insomnia began, he had complained to his parents about the new medication making him sick. Without question, his mother flushed the bottle's contents down the toilet and called Dr. Adjei. In a firm, raised voice, she laid into the man. The medication meant to give her *sweet rabbit* a peaceable night's rest had almost put him in an early grave.

But even after he stopped taking the medication, there was no change. The tension between his parents continued to intensify, and August knew he was the one to blame. If he were born normal, then there would be no shouting throughout all hours of the day and night. There would be no impromptu business trips that he knew his father used as a form of escapism. There would be no drinking and venom-laced words hurled at him in his father's absence by the woman who a day later would present him with a burnt offering of pancakes as a token of apology.

Because the night before, *mommy wasn't herself*, and *it was the alcohol talking*. It was always the alcohol that made her tell the ugly truth. It was the alcohol that made her kick his wheelchair out of reach whenever August decided he had heard enough of her drivel and attempted to retreat. No, he was to sit his ass right there and listen to what she had to say because he *owed* her that much. And she never did stop until she'd broken him down completely.

The darkness persisted. The whispers persisted.

What frightened August most of all was the knowing. Each night there was something there with him in the void. Something that drew closer every time he shut his eyes to rest. The something that chipped away at him bit-by-bit, piece-by-piece.

"August," Seko said. "Look at me." Her tone softened like a parent seeking to pull the whole truth from a child's half-lie. The problem with that notion is that August was telling the whole truth. Understanding a solitary whisper was one thing, but a legion of whispering voices was impossible to comprehend. "You need not be afraid."

"Sure, I'm scared. But not for the reason you think." August said. "And I'm not lying either. I can't remember because I never know what they're saying. When I hear them, it's like listening to a pit of hissing snakes."

Seko did not divert her eyes and stared at him expectantly and without blinking. "Go on then. I am listening."

"What? Did you not hear what I just said? I don't know anything."

"If Master August says he doesn't know, then he doesn't know. We're wasting time. While we sit here wagging our chins, they could be sending more of those golem creatures." Reginald said, his irritation matching his ward's.

Seko held up a finger, signaling for the manservant to wait. "I'm listening, August. You need to talk to me."

August became increasingly uncomfortable under her unwavering stare and was suddenly cognizant her hand still held his. Then there was that sound. A sound akin to a clock's rhythmic ticking. A scratching sound that he could not only hear but feel. Sandpaper: coarse, loud, and growing louder in the ear.

He looked down and saw the woman's thumb stroking the back of his hand. It swept from left to right, steady like the pendulum of a metronome. August tried jerking away, but his hand was caught and squeezed, prompting the manservant to lurch forward across the table. He flinched seeing the collision coming and consequently dropped his eyes to the blue sapphire pendant hanging around Seko's neck on silver chain.

The pendant spun unnaturally. First winding the chain in one direction and then the other and did so continuously without losing momentum. The stone itself was mesmerizing, sparkled brilliantly with a light that seemed otherworldly, and the speed at which it spun increased.

Out the corner of August's eye (to his right), he saw

Reggie's face full of fury. To his left, the open fireplace. He noticed that although they were in motion, both man and fire had slowed to a crawl. It was as if someone had altered their playback speed in much the same way he would the characters in one of his virtual reality simulators.

August felt terrible pressure on his brain and wondered if he was having a seizure. Something he hadn't experienced since age thirteen. The scratching sound resumed its steady, hypnotic beat, more pronounced than before. His eyelids grew heavy, and he knew there was more to it than the day's fatigue catching up with him. He fought it. He didn't want to sleep. He may not have known what awaited him on the other side in the pitch-black void, but knew whatever it was, was hungry and eager to take more bites out of him.

"What are you doing to me?" August slurred like a drunkard. The more he resisted the overwhelming urge to shut his eyes, the more incapacitated he became, to the point where his head felt like a lead weight.

"I need you to sleep," Seko said.

"I can't. I'll die. You're killing me. Please, stop." August pleaded. The fear in his voice unmistakable. He felt rough hands hold his face and the thumbs brushing away his tears.

"Hush now. Rest those weary eyes."

CHAPTER 13

THE MOON WAS BUT A sliver in the frigid night sky and becoming thinner. Clouds burdened with snow loomed overhead. A handheld AM/FM radio played commercials in the absence of popular Motown disc jockey of yesteryear, Alvin in the AM, covering for the Grown and Sexy Hour. The listener was urged to pick up a Hot-N-Ready pizza for just five bucks at their local Little Caesars, told to get in on Mr. Alan's two for fifty sale on winter boots, and informed that no job was too big or too small for Father & Son's Construction Company.

One hundred acres of mostly wooded land made it easy to hunker down undetected. But much was left to be desired when it came to a person finding ways to be entertained. The trespasser wasn't bored but restless. For over an hour now, the two humanoid forms standing at the edge of the makeshift camp hadn't moved. They were still, like scarecrows, except for their hooded white cloaks, which billowed whenever a strong wind gusted.

Together the pair stood with their backs to the fire, their hands intertwined, and their masked faces pointed at the lodge in the distance. The house was no more than a bleak silhouette in the night. Of this, the trespasser made certain. Had to. Because after what transpired three days ago, there was no margin for error.

It had been a bitter pill to swallow. Months of meticulous planning turned on its head in a matter of minutes. Not to mention one of their strongest assets was compromised. The colossus was a combat-ready golem specifically cultivated to dispatch the boy's protector. Ula poured weeks into its creation. She was the one who spoke to the trees and pulled from the veil the gifts bestowed onto her by the Green Woman. The Pale amplified her gifts tenfold.

Ula had taken much from the veil. Too much. And in return, it had taken almost all of her, leaving the girl bedridden for days after completing the task. The trespasser understood. They all understood. To receive from the veil, one must be willing to give, and Ula gave a portion of her soul for every golem she'd birthed. As a result, she had become a waif: thin and sickly.

If it were at all possible, such a burden would have never been placed on the girl. But it wasn't possible to carry out their plans without Ula. Matilda, hard as she tried, could not penetrate the manservant's psyche. Doing so would have made things much easier by simply turning the butler's mind on itself. Matilda had speculated the man could be veil-touched in some way without even knowing it. Rare but not unfounded.

In their hubris, it was foolish to believe they had made it this far without detection. They had moved slowly, meticulously in carrying out their plans, and yet the little blackbirds somehow managed to see them. How long had they been watching? What did they know? Had they only sent just the one? If so, then why just one? A scout, perhaps. See. Run. Tell. But the scout wouldn't be telling anything because said scout was buried beneath no less than a foot of snow and unequivocally deceased.

The trespasser did find some irony in the situation. Using a lesser gateway stone (which grants its wielder the ability to travel great distances in a matter of minutes), they had sent the colossus to spy on their prey and make sure things were safe for them to follow in its footsteps. However, upon its arrival, someone attacked the colossus almost instantaneously. A spy sent to eliminate a spy. The little bird had succeeded too in what Ula described as an act of sheer desperation. The blackbird forfeited her life, fatally stabbed not once but twice through and through by the colossus, and life spilled out of her body in a river of blood hot enough to melt ice.

This little bird. This Magpie. In a last stand, while having the life rung out of her by constricting vines, pulled the pin of an incendiary grenade. The Green Woman's greatest enemy next to man was fire, and the colossus had burned in a baptism of flame.

After much debate, the three arrived a day later to take inventory of the damage done. Ula and Matilda were reluctant to go because the colossus's destruction meant there was no way to know what awaited them on the other side of the gateway. The trespasser had assured them that scouts generally appear when someone knew very little and wanted to know more. A calculated risk, really. If wrong and Magpie did know what they were up to, then the Foxx estate would be blanketed in a murder of black darlings eager to please their master in a misguided sense of honor.

The trespasser had not been wrong. They found what they came for: two corpses, one made of flesh and blood and the other of birch wood, ash, and black earth. The flesh and blood they discarded into a natural trench and the inclement weather had done the rest. Collecting the colossus's remains had been a joint effort.

"Do you want to tell it, or should I?" A bitter voice split the darkness.

"I can speak for myself." A smaller voice said, sounding like a whisper on the wind.

At the camp's edge, the two figures stirred to life. They approached the fire. The tallest rooted herself before the trespasser while the other sat on a snow-crusted stump adopting an exhausted posture.

"Ula fucked up. We didn't get the boy." Matilda said, her masked face turned down at the trespasser. Carved in the ashen mask was a beautiful, stoic face belonging to the goddess of dreams. The eyes were swan eyes, graceful and wise, and across her forehead a crown of stars, three on either side of a spherical moon. The moon was near total darkness and mirrored the sky above. The tiny visible crescent gave off a pale celestial glow.

"You think it acceptable to belittle family?" The trespasser said with a voice that sounded like coarse gravel.

"What? Did you not hear me? We don't have the boy." Matilda seethed.

"I can see that. Perhaps it is you who did not hear me."

Matilda's head drooped like a scolded child. "No. Of course, I don't think that."

"Good. Because if one of us fails, then we all fail. Now apologize to your sister."

"My apologies Ula. I was angry. Scared."

"It's all right," Ula said. The cold had set into her narrow bones. She hugged herself by the fire to keep from shaking apart. "But Matilda's right. It's my fault. I made a mistake. You see, the blackbird is alive."

Hearing the revelation, the trespasser said nothing. They sat motionless as always whenever the two decided to dump a heavy problem into their lap. The trespasser chewed on Ula's words, found them to have the unpleasant consistency and taste of rubbery fatback, and despite the masks covering their faces, the trespasser knew their eyes were full of fear and desperation.

"We shouldn't have come. We needed more time to prepare and more time for Ula to rest. We cannot do this now." Matilda said.

"There won't be another time." The trespasser said. They were angry at them, but their voice reflected that anger no more than the blank mask they wore. Through the mask's black slits for eyes, the trespasser watched the campfire. To give way to anger would be catastrophic. Ula, who was sensitive and responded well to positive reinforcement, would instantly go to tears. Matilda, on the other hand, tended to shut down and become withdrawn whenever she felt attacked. So the trespasser chose their next words carefully.

"Tonight, the moon will be born anew. We know this is a once-in-a-lifetime occurrence for us. Without the lifegiver, our bodies are not long for this world, and in another hundred years, if we so choose to resign ourselves to such a fate, our bones will be buried in unmarked graves or dust scattered across the earth. Either way, time will not remember us in a world where man strays further from the old ways with each passing day in favor of his technological advancements. The world will turn right on. If we don't do this thing, then our family will never be made whole."

Ula and Matilda listened in silence. Ula stopped trying to draw heat into her body, and Matilda backed away and seated herself on a bulky camouflaged rucksack.

"What do we do?" Ula asked.

"Tell me what happened." The trespasser said.

Ula recounted the events that took place at the lodge. The trespasser listened. Ula had made a snap judgment decision between choosing to eliminate the unconscious blackbird or grabbing the boy and fleeing. At the time, she had been manipulating two lesser golems at once to better assess the situation within the lodge's walls.

As it turned out, the little bird was both a blessing in disguise and a curse. A blessing because her presence directly resulted in the manservant separating from his ward and a curse because there were now two highly trained killers instead of one. When the manservant managed to overpower the first golem Ula had panicked. On the bright side, the aging military veteran had been wounded.

"There's something else you should know," Matilda said with newfound optimism.

"Enlighten me." The trespasser said.

"When Ula and I were mentally linked, I was able to influence the butler's mind. I know his past. I know what haunts him. I can make him see those things. Live those things." The gifts bestowed on Matilda by the veil gave her the unique ability to peer inside other people's minds. She could see their past and present, manipulate their thoughts and memories, subjecting them to a fully realized psychosis where dreams and reality were indistinguishable. But like Ula's gifts, Matilda's too was not without consequence.

"That's good, Matilda. That's *real* good."

It was thought that a supernatural force blocked the butler's mind from manipulation. Now they knew distance was to blame all along. A huge victory since the boy's dreams were off-limits to them, protected by an unforeseen force. The best Matilda could do was disrupt his sleep pattern, depriving the body of the rest it needed, causing it to wilt. No medicine could combat that.

"See?" The trespasser rose. "There isn't reason to be afraid. You thought we failed, but the two of you brought us a victory. They may know what we want, and they will protect that boy with all they have, but they don't know why we want him. And thanks to Ula, we were able to scout them from a distance without revealing ourselves. Now's the time, sisters. Now we take what belongs to us."

Matilda stood up, unzipping the rucksack. An assortment of automatic and semi-automatic firearms, magazines, ammunition boxes, and bladed weapons protruded out.

"But sister, I'm afraid I'm of no further use. I cannot create another golem." Ula said. Her bird-like frame made her look as if a stiff breeze would carry her off.

"You won't need to. Isn't that right, Matilda?" Matilda nodded. The trespasser's head turned towards the barren treetops that stretched to a sky devoid almost entirely of light. Something was watching them. Whatever it was, was massive and the trespasser would not have seen it if not for the shimmering bits of crystalized snow outlining the being's hulking form. "Go on now. We won't be long behind you." Said the trespasser, gripping tight the beaded necklace fastened about their neck. The symbols marking each bead pulsed lightning white.

No sooner than the words left the trespasser's mouth did a wind rush them with such tremendous force the surrounding trees bowed to the ground. Ula and Matilda were knocked off their feet. Snow whipped around them violently, and the trespasser fell on bended knee, palms pressed to the ground to keep from toppling over. The hood on their head blew free, and a train of fiery red hair rode the gale.

The handheld AM/FM radio crackled. The disc jockey's voice rumbled like thunder.

"This winter weather has been something else. Two days in a row of back-to-back snow. That's two feet of snow in two days, baby. I know some of you couples are frustrated, trapped at home, and you don't know what to do with yourselves. Well, that's not entirely true. Some of y'all better slow down before you come out of this storm with more than you went in with, if you know what I'm saying. It won't be long now, though. Looks like mother nature is going to cut us a little slack tonight. And for all you single ladies out there with nothing to hold on to but a glass of Chardonnay and a couple of D-Cell batteries, Alvin, your chocolate teddy bear, has got you covered. A quick shout out to one of our sponsors. The folks over at the Samson's Salt Company who are working around the clock to clear our highways and byways. If Samson's Salt can't melt it, then nobody can. Speaking of melting, let's heat things up a bit with a little D'Angelo. This one's off that two-thousand joint Voodoo. I hope you're ready for The Root."

CHAPTER 14

WHAT IS DARKNESS? NINE TIMES out of ten, if you go up to a person on the streets and ask them whether or not they are afraid of the dark, the answer will be yes. To many, darkness is the fear of the unknown. A place where past traumas reside out-of-sight and out-of-mind, festering and waiting, knowing their victims will undoubtedly return to that insufferable place to relive the nightmare all over again, whether it be by a trigger or a lapse in judgment while traveling down the road of nostalgia and at the crossroads the brain went left when it should have gone right.

For August, he preferred darkness as his choice of escapism. When he closed his eyes to sleep, he knew darkness would comfort him, and when he opened them again, something worthwhile would be waiting for him on the other side. He would bask in the weightlessness of time and space where he experienced an indescribable awareness of being alive and what that truly meant. But he no longer felt this way about sleep, about the darkness.

Unlike before, the darkness no longer blossomed into beautiful landscapes inhabited by creatures and a people whose existence in the real world was relegated to works of fiction. When he shut his eyes now, the experience was on par with a small animal placed inside a box, and the lid sealed shut. It suffocated him. Then that simultaneous feeling of being alone and not alone. The disembodied amalgam of voices whispering strange and unfamiliar things gnawed at his consciousness like rats and made peace impossible to obtain.

August felt damp. No, soaked through to the bone. His eyes open but, he could not see a thing. When he tried to breathe, no air entered his lungs to the point where he began to gasp, choke and sputter. Despite his clouded mind, he came to the startling realization that he was drowning and impulsively tried to push himself up onto his hands and knees. It worked.

Still, August's chest burned as he continued to cough, hacking up what felt like buckets of water at a time. His hair, normally parted and gelled to perfection, hung forward, matting to his face and blinding him. He tossed his head back, panting. He looked around taking stock of his surroundings. However, the first thing August noticed didn't come through sight but through his nostrils. His insides lurched in response to the repulsive stench that hung in the air, but his stomach had nothing left to give. Whatever it was, was one hundred times worse than any roadkill he and Reggie had ever encountered on any motorway. Which begged the question, where had he wound up?

A buzzing familiarity rattled around in his skull. August last remembered Seko telling him to sleep. Now he sat on his heels in the middle of what appeared to be a lake. Or perhaps it once was. The water level so low it would be impossible to drown unless you found yourself face down and unconscious, which he had. Trees and rolling hills enclosed the lake on all sides. His eyes stung, finding it difficult to adjust to the unearthly vermilion haze that washed over the lands far as the eye could see.

August got to his feet. He shielded his eyes with a hand and began walking with no sense of direction. He moved ordinarily and unassisted the way he always did in dreams. The further he moved away from the lake's center, the more apparent the oppressive force hovering about him became. Calve-high water rippled away from him, looking like sheets of diluted blood. His legs grew heavier with each step. He wanted to place the blame on fatigue but, deep down, knew this couldn't be true. This thick miasma, in combination with his legs unwillingness to function, came across like a warning. A primal trigger ingrained in man's DNA throughout the ages that shouted for the body to be still and the ears to listen. August did neither.

He did not stop walking until his bare toes sank into the cool mud at the shoreline. His eyes happened upon a scene that made him hold his breath, and the blood in his veins ran cold. How he hadn't heard them until now was a mystery. Even while sloshing through the water, their guttural cries and nonstop squawking should have cut across the lake to his ears, dominating all other competing sounds. August hadn't even expected there to be a beach. It manifested so quickly, and matter-of-factly, his brain hadn't processed the transition at all. Like lag or jerky procedurally generated textures in a video game running on a shitty processor. Yet the beach existed all the same, and so did they.

August knew he had come face-to-face with the source of the rancid stench permeating around and through him. The ball in his throat bobbed with the compulsion to vomit. His eyes stung. Never in his fucking life had he experienced fear like this before. They swarmed the beach. Birds that dwarfed him in height and their white feathers soiled crimson by their feeding frenzy.

He remembered the elves from his dreams and how he'd fought alongside them many times, beating back undead hordes. August remembered them now because the ageless wonders lay strewn across the white sand. They were barely indistinguishable from butchered meat in a slaughterhouse. In petrified horror, he witnessed a pair of overgrown avians fight over a bundle of intestines spilling out of a bloated corpse. What made matters worse were the ones who still had faces he knew by name. Whatever doubts lingered in August's mind concerning the sharpness of the creatures' elongated, serrated beaks were dispelled when an elf's torso was snipped free from its lower half. His dream had become a nightmare.

August did not know what was worse, the shrill squawking or the droning flies. Both constant. How did this happen? He wanted to wake up. A terrifying reptilian hiss jarred him from his stupor. He jerked his head in time to spot a monstrous carnivorous bird charging right at him. Already towering over him, it raised its wings, boasting a wingspan no less than twenty feet. He reared back in fright, narrowly avoiding its jagged beak.

He was so close to the creature he could see its eyes: white with nary a pupil in sight. Was it blind? Nocturnal? There was no time to contemplate these things as he was driven backward by snapping beak and giant beating wings. The spectacle drew additional feathered monstrosities. They hissed and jockeyed, competing to be first to sever his limbs and devour them. He knew if he didn't move, he would die.

August turned on his heels and tore off running down the beach. He dared not look back. He didn't have to. Before long, a cold shadow sailed over him. Angry hisses rained from above, transforming into confident, intimidating squawks. The sky beast's winged shadow blocked the red sky, grew larger as it descended on him at an alarming speed. He ran faster, harder, lungs on the verge of exploding. His legs tightened. The muscles in his stomach knotted.

Knowing not what else to do, he threw up his hands to shield his head. He knew this would do nothing. The razor-sharp talons homing in on him would tear clean through his soft flesh.

August screamed.

In a blur, a feathered monstrosity rocketed past him, and with it came a wind so powerful the surrounding sand parted like the fabled Red Sea. Dust clouds obscured his vision. He went from running to staggering, not knowing left from right or forward from backward. He could hear them squawking, hissing, and gigantic wings beating the sky. But what blindsided him was charred flesh on the wind.

The dust storm began to relent, and through it, although barely, he saw something in the distance. Something that shimmered; twinkled like a diamond. Its indigo glow, a defiant beacon that cut through the oppressive red. As it drew nearer, a person's form took shape, their arms pointing with purpose first in one direction and then another. August felt the person was somehow responsible for the drastic temperature change. The dank atmosphere had become faint-worthy rippling heat waves.

August stopped dead in his tracks. He watched the approaching figure with uncertainty, and for a split second, had forgotten why he started running in the first place. A shrill cry overhead reminded him. He changed directions, set one foot in front of the other, and went nowhere other than straight up. He felt numbness in his right shoulder. A dull throbbing his mind couldn't quite comprehend. Looking at it, he felt nausea wash over him. Inflamed muscle and tendons burst forth like ground meat. The culprit, an oversized talon, hooked through flesh and carried him by bone.

Pain flared in tremors and fever sweat drenched him. Looking down, he saw the ground shrinking beneath him. Looking up, he saw white feathers and dark blood. In the places where there were no feathers, open wounds festered. They smelled foul. He thought about his great grandfather's care home. Thought about how sickness and death clung to the walls there. This is what that smell was but magnified. It was sunbaked death left on the side of the road to rot.

The wounds pulsed, yellow pus writhed, swimming with hundreds, if not thousands of maggots. Some fell away in clumps. August dry heaved. He imagined dying as the feathered monstrosity picked the flesh from his bones. What would his mother think? She would want to protect him. She would shout at the top of her lungs for someone, anyone, to do something and unintentionally bring damnation onto herself. He believed her heart was almost always in the right place, but that made her no less a fool.

As for his father? The man would look on with quiet indifference. His shoulders becoming lighter the further the winged monstrosity carried his son—his burden—away.

Tears burned August's eyes. *I'm not a rabbit*, he thought. *I'm not helpless.*

Here in the dream, he had been brave, strong, and never died. In the waking world, he felt he had died a thousand deaths. Did death carry over from here to there? He wasn't willing to find out. Bravery had nothing to do with the decision, for it was fight or flight that hammered his heart. August mustered his strength, fisted his left hand, and drove his knuckles into the terror bird's clutching talon with all his might. Bone struck what felt like an iron plate, and nerves screamed out in hand and shoulder.

Just as there was no honor among thieves, there was no such thing as a free and clear meal among scavengers. He beat his knuckles bloody, bicycled his legs, unaware of the second undead horror gliding towards him. And if it couldn't have *all* of him, then it would take half. He saw it too little too late, razor-sharp talons thrust forward, aimed to grab, aimed to separate his lower from his upper. August laughed. The sound was miserable. Miserable because he knew he wouldn't open his eyes again in the waking world.

This creature, this reanimated thing, this terror bird, this opportunist with razor-sharp talons and serrated beak went rigid then dropped stone cold dead out of the sky. All at once, August's face and chest were made hot, wet, and sticky. Fresh blood, brain matter, and hard beak flecks clung to him. His body remained tense, anticipating an impact that never came, and before he could ask why the answer appeared right in front of him.

An indigo light beam shot past his dangling form. The beam's splash heat instantaneously dried and hardened exploded flesh and blood to his face. He followed its trajectory, watched the blazing bright beam incinerate one of his captor's wings.

The feathered monstrosity shrieked. Shocked and desperate, it flapped its remaining gigantic wing. They spiraled, losing altitude rapidly, then plummeted straight down. August was stuck, hooked on the claw protruding through his shoulder as he watched the ground rush up at him. His adrenaline kicked in. He thrashed, jerked, and tore at the creature's claw. It was too late.

With a resounding crunch, the feathered monstrosity crash-landed on its neck, flipped onto its back, and tumbled along the shoreline. August was flung free. Sand scraped and tore away his skin as he went head over ass like a tumbleweed. The back of his head smacked what felt like the ground, but it was a patch of dry yellow grass that broke his fall and forced the air from his lungs.

His world spun like a top. Everything hurt, but he was alive. His eyes went in and out of focus. To his right, he saw a lake of blood. To his left, a feast for the flies and maggots. Black smoke was on the wind. A figure hovered above him darker than shadow. Spherical blue light emitted where the figure's chest should have been; painful and blinding then soft and calming.

August gave in to the shock, to the pain. His eyes rolled white.

"I got you, August. I got you."

MORNING. IT FELT like morning. Chilly, unlike the coziness that comes with lying down the night prior. He cracked his eyes open. The world was still but fuzzy, and he knew he was not alone. An early riser himself, Reggie, had no doubt come to set their morning ritual in motion. First, they would begin with a trip to the loo, followed by some exercises to get the blood flowing and a shower after that. Afterward, he would eat a light breakfast consisting of fresh fruit and warm oats.

"Sun's up already?" August groaned.

"Here there is no sun." A voice rasped, the words sobering.

He sat bolt upright. His right shoulder, along with the rest of his body, protested. Looking at his shoulder, he expected to see inflamed flesh evacuating his skin like a burst sausage casing. To his surprise, there was no wound.

"You took a nasty fall." The voice said, sounding more familiar now. "I used almost all the pendant's magic to heal you."

"I'm still dreaming?" The question rhetorical. He looked

around and saw he was no longer on the beach. Coarse grass cushioned his buttocks, and an enclosure of bare, wilted trees surrounded him. Through them, he could see the deceptively calm white beach and rolling hills in the distance.

"This is no dream."

"What do you mean? I'm sleep, aren't I?"

"I think you know better than that. I had my suspicions about you, but until now, I was not certain."

"No, no, no. This is a dream. A nightmare. I want to wake up."

"Stop playing the fool. Or perhaps it suits you being the helpless rabbit skirting the pot?"

"*Don't* call me that!"

"Then stop behaving as such. We don't have the time."

August regarded the thing seated beneath the dead tree. Where one would expect a human's head to be, there was none. In its place sat a black human-proportioned bird's head, its beady black eyes reflecting the vermillion haze that dominated the landscape. Its broad shoulders consisted of sharp-looking black and white feathers resembling pauldrons.

"Seko, is it really you?"

"Who else would I be?"

"You look—"

"Everyone looks different when they travel," Seko said, the light in the pendant around her neck dwindling. "We don't have time."

"You're saying… you're suggesting this is all real?"

"How many mornings have you awoke to find yourself sore, bruised, and cut without explanation? How many mornings have these findings left you with a sense of déjà vu?"

Many, he thought, but didn't want to believe it. He had been under the impression the minor scrapes and bruises had come from the rigors of his day-to-day existence. Now Seko was telling him his dreams were more than vivid imagination and rapid eye movement.

"There is a long-standing theory suggesting people live multiple lives without ever knowing it," Seko said. "Says that when we shut our eyes in one world, we open them in another. You have been here before, yes?"

August nodded, bewildered panic flickering in his eyes. "I have, but it's been a while. On account of the insomnia, I mean. Everything's changed. It's *all* wrong. I don't understand what's happened here. And how're you with me?"

Seko clasped the pendant. "Do not ask what you already know. As for this place? I suspect on your last visit, something followed you. That something, I think, has been awaiting your return." She pointed an onyx finger to the sky.

"What? If that's true, then why the hell would you bring me here?"

"Look up."

He tilted his head back and looked. Through scrawny naked tree branches, he saw five spheres hanging in the sky. They were moons in a ring formation, or so they appeared to be, but much smaller than Earth's moon. Each one was a deep vermillion hue, ripe inverted blood oranges, that if squeezed, would flood the landscape in an ocean of red.

"Everything here is either dead or dying, and those diseased rats with wings are a plague set loose on this place.

We are here for the truth, August. Because without it, we will die. *You* will die." Seko said.

"I've told you everything already."

"If by everything, you mean nothing."

"What do you want from me? I don't know what the whispers say. I don't know anything."

"There it is. You *are* just a scared little rabbit."

"I said not to call me that."

"I call it by what my ears hear and my eyes see, a scared little rabbit hiding in the bush."

August was on his feet before he knew it, his jaw clenched and brows creased. "Shut your mouth." He said.

"There is nothing worse than a coward who hides the truth to spare his pride."

Her words slapped him hard across the face. Stunned him, but not for long. Blinded by rage, his feet raced like the wind closing the distance between himself and the magpie. She exploded from the ground in a blur of black and white, rising higher and higher, towering over August at seven foot even. A hand that was not a hand seized him by the throat, hoisted him in the air.

"Let go!" He growled, thrashed, and kicked, but Seko held him at arm's length.

"What are you afraid of? Does your life or the butler's life mean nothing to you?" A magnificent pair of wings unfolded from Seko's back, each feather a black mirror, and in them, August saw his fear reflected.

"I'm not sure what's real," His words shocked him as he struggled to speak with the vice clamped around his throat.

This was a truth he hadn't shared with anyone before. "Wouldn't you be afraid if you were me? You know how people walk into a room and forget why they're there? It's not like that for me. I forget the whole room. I see things that aren't there, and it keeps getting worse. I tell myself it's part of it, you know? Because I'm dying. Or did you not know that?"

"Tell me what you saw."

August blinked back tears as he was placed on his feet. "Different things. One time I saw women on a beach. They were chanting something, but I don't remember the words."

"Think, August. You must remember."

"I... Something about the veil. They mentioned a king. I remember seeing a deer, a black one. I think they were praying to it."

The magpie studied him with an expressionless face, its yellow-orange eyes unblinking. "Do you see this?" Of course, he did. Even with its light diminished, the sapphire gem was hard to miss. The stone had taken on the rhythm of a weak heartbeat. "Synthesized veil essence. Not as potent as the real thing but useful when combating the supernatural. I've exhausted most of it to save my own life before you and the butler found me buried in the snow. Then I used more to hijack your consciousness and bring us here."

August's pupils dilated. His shoulders, which had been tense, drooped.

"A little more to mend your shoulder," Seko continued. "Now the time has come to open your mind to me. Tell me, boy. Beyond the whispers, what do you hear?"

He stood there unmoving and unspeaking. His pupils

so dilated his eyes could be mistaken for black. When he opened his mouth, the voice that came out was cracked and far away. "Can you not hear them? The beat of four-thousand hooves pounding the earth? The riders died for Him in the Great Conquest, and he rewarded them, raised them from the battlefields, the tombs, and the pyres. Again they ride, their voices shouting glory and exaltation to Him as they cut down His enemies like wheat in a field."

"Who is he? Tell me the black deer's name."

"Aren't you listening? Haven't you been paying attention?" Tears flowed down his cheeks. "He who is merciful to His subjects. He who sits low and looks high. The Light that conquers the Dark. Void Walker. The Pale One. The Pale King. King of Pestilence. Praise thy holy name!"

Bolts of lightning set the sky ablaze and thunder shook the ground.

Seko flinched, gripping the pendant tight. At the center of the five crimson moons, a crescent moon began to manifest. "I see you, demon. You are no god. Time to go home, August. Time to come back to me."

August fell to his knees, threw up his arms, and cried out. "No, I can't. I won't. You wanted to see Him. You *must* see Him. He drinks the blood of princes to open the gate because they have the blood of kings in their veins. They spill the blood of red and blood of white, and the white is the sperm because the day has changed, and in this day, no man guards his seed. Our world is made ripe for Him. I am a prince, but he will make me His princess. Do you know what that means? He will drink my blood to open the gate and everything his light touches...

Everything His light touches. Everything His light touches. Everything His light touches. Everything His light touches will *be* His."

"August. I know you hear me, boy. Come back to me right now!" Seko demanded. She squeezed the pendant, its indigo glow all but depleted.

"I remember the words." August said. He grinned wide. "One eye on the stars. One eye on the veil. One eye on man. One eye on hell."

For each line recited, a moon of the pre-existing five moons turned over. Each one revealed itself to be a sentient eye. White beams opened like vicious spotlights eviscerating grass, pitiful trees, and bringing the remaining lake water to a roaring boil.

"One eye turned towards the heavens." He said. A bolt of lightning cracked the sky wide open, and bestial wind howled. The crescent moon grew in diameter. The ground trembled and quaked, but this time thunder was not the cause.

In the distance, horses surmounted the surrounding hills, four-thousand hooves pounding the dirt and kicking up tufts of grass. Saddles seated riders originating from dynasties recorded in no book written by man. They wore fine garments and armor weathered by time, shallow graves, and some scorched by fire. Their skin, which was a ghastly pale, was pulled tight against sinew muscle and exposed bleached-white bone. On the brewing storm, death rode with them.

August watched the riders approach with the gleefulness of a religious fanatic who'd given up their last in exchange for salvation. He welcomed them with open arms and a smile not suited for his otherwise stoic face: a twisted, toothy smile, gleaming saliva drizzling down his chin and neck. He heard them then, the voices, no longer whispering but speaking clearly.

"Love Him," one said.

"Accept Him," another said.

"You are both door and key," said the third.

The words, although simple, filled him with a sense of purpose. A wonderful feeling unlike any he'd experienced that washed away his woes of inadequacy. He opened his mouth to speak, to pledge his heart, soul, flesh, and blood to the Pale King, and just as his lips parted, fingers seized him by the back of the head.

"I said it is time to leave," Seko shouted over the thundering horses. She stripped the pendant off, pressed it to his forehead. August's world exploded into flocking blackbirds. They shrouded him in darkness.

CHAPTER 15

TIME. TIME OPERATES DIFFERENTLY ON a realm-by-realm basis. Something the manservant, Reginald Ristil, wouldn't know anything about. All he sees is what is right in front of him: the here and now. He witnesses his ward snatch away from the stranger's touch. She takes the boy's hand again. He squirms, unable to dislodge her grip a second time. She proceeds to invade his ward's personal space, their faces grow closer, and he thinks she is about to do the unspeakable. It all happens within the blink of an eye.

Reginald threw himself across the coffee table. The sturdy mahogany did not budge, clipping him at the shins, and sent him crashing against Seko instead of tackling her. Either way, his large hands found their way around her throat as they spilled to the floor, and all one hundred and four kilograms of him came down on top of her.

Anyone else would have been devastated by such a collision, and although Seko did appear disoriented, Reginald couldn't shake the feeling she had been expecting him. He wasn't wrong.

She grabbed his wrists and tucked her chin to prevent total asphyxiation, a reaction not at all uncommon for someone getting throttled. What was out of the ordinary was the sudden sharp pain Reginald felt in his sides. The big man thought himself stabbed, but it was Seko's heels striking him in a series of well-placed kicks. His kidneys and recently bandaged wound screamed for mercy. He tore himself away from her, or so that had been the idea.

Seko was every bit as strong as she appeared, held him firmly by the wrists while using her feet to push his legs out from under him in a fluid push-pull motion, breaking Reginald's grip on her throat. He grimaced, staring up into the brown face illuminated by the fire's light. In her eyes, he saw an eerie calm. He knew what he had done wrong. The woman was at home on her back, and he had impulsively and arrogantly thrown himself right into her guard.

It was too little too late. Reginald was already forced halfway down her body, his arms hyperextended. It had been years since he'd participated in any real grappling. In his heyday, he'd been quite good. Now, although physically imposing, it was clear to him more than ever that he was out of shape and outclassed. This was further emphasized when Seko rolled him and her thighs wrapped around his neck, cutting off the blood flow to his head.

"Stop this. I am not the enemy." Seko said.

Reginald could see spots floating in his eyes. He thought he heard laughing, deranged and unrelenting. His eyes grew heavy and he could feel the abyss coming on. Seko turned him loose.

"The traveler has moved on his belly for long, He once had legs but now they're gone. For all eternity does He stretch, but if He curls up be prepared to retch. Your bones will twist, creak, and pop, you won't be able to scream and He won't stop. Once you're still and you think that's it, He unhinges His jaws and you see the pit." August laughed, grinning ear to ear.

Reginald sat up, half falling over as he did, and rubbed at his bruised Adam's apple. His ego, too, was bruised, but that was unimportant. Seeing his ward's face, he didn't recognize it. The skin around August's mouth stretched to a hideous grin. In his mind, no amount of happiness in the world could bring a person to grin like that. What he saw was pure lunacy.

"What have you done?" Reginald coughed, staggering to his feet. "What have you done to him?"

Seko did not answer. She was either ignoring him or did not hear him over the boy's hysterical laughter. She hastily undid the silver chain, clasping it around August's lean neck. The laughter died.

"Well? I suggest you start telling me something." Reginald frowned, witnessing his charge slump forward unconscious. There would be no more acting on impulse from him. No second chance for further surprises. No more secrets and talking in riddles. He may not have been what he once was but on his feet and focused made him plenty dangerous for anyone foolish enough to face him head-on.

In his peripheral, he noted the coffee table. More importantly, the strange knife there along with the pistol, though it was furthest from reach. He stepped towards Seko and she back. Their eyes darted to the table, and they both went for it, but Reginald got to the knife first.

"You know not what you are doing." Seko said.

"Here's what I do know," Reginald said. "My ward's unconscious, and you're responsible. Before that, you whispered something to him. I don't know what you said, but whatever it was," He shook his head, inverting the knife in his grip. "What did you do?"

"Does it matter what I say? You are standing with one foot in the river and the other on dry land."

"What does that even mean?"

"It means it will take all of us, *all* of you if we plan to see sunrise."

"You think I'm not all here? I may not subscribe to all this supernatural bullshit, but like Master August said, I can't deny what I've seen."

"Good. Because this supernatural bullshit subscribes to you. Believe me, if I wanted to harm you or the boy, it would already be."

"Alright. Fill in the blanks for me."

"I know what wants the boy. He told me so himself when I went into his dream. A demon that fancies itself a god."

"Demon?"

"Yes. He has been called Void Walker, King of Pestilence, the Light that conquers the Dark."

With each name Seko spoke, Reginald felt a growing

uneasiness drag up his back, kneading its hooks into his already taunt shoulders. The room felt like it dropped several degrees in temperature. In fact, it had. He told himself the reason as to why was a logical one, that when the power first went out, there had still been sunlight, and now with the sun vanished from the sky, the temperature was subject to change. He needed to check the circuit breaker, something he would have already done under normal circumstances. But to leave August's side again was out of the question.

"I thought demons were all about darkness," Reginald said. "You say this one is the light that conquers the dark. What does that mean?"

"Darkness is often misinterpreted to fit a given narrative. In children's fairy tales, darkness is used to inspire fear, hopelessness, obedience even. Light is used to signify courage and triumph. The universe was born out of darkness, so how can it be wicked? Truth is darkness is no more inherently wicked than light is inherently good." Seko said. "Yes, there are times when wickedness lurks in the shadows, but most of the time, it hides in plain sight: like the uncle who gropes his niece at the family dinner or the neighbor who is championed a pillar of his community while the bodies pile up in his basement. Darkness and light are merely tools."

Reginald adopted a thoughtful expression. He spoke slowly to mask his unease. "And this demon's light?"

"Everything his light touches burns and dies then is brought back changed, warped." Seko's eyes went to the knife. "That knife was not meant for you. It was meant for the boy. You see, the demon cannot pass through the veil just because he wishes it to be so. He can only be summoned through sacrifice."

"What makes Master August so special?"

"I don't know. I was hoping you could tell me. What do you know about the family you serve?"

Reginald stepped forward. He was so close that all he had to do was make one quick slash with the knife, and Seko's throat would open in a fountain of blood. To his surprise and hers too, judging by the look on her face, he handed her the knife. "Apparently not as much as I thought I did." He said, taking the boy into his arms.

"Nothing at all? No strange happenings?"

"No. Unless you count his grandfather's unhealthy obsession with antique model ships. Seems the older he gets the more he hoards the past."

"What about a black deer?"

"A what?"

"The boy claims he saw women worshipping a black deer. A being with many names can have many faces."

He hesitated a moment remembering the painting with the dancing women, the buck, and the bleeding sky. "Sounds like witchcraft."

"Of that, I have no doubt."

"I've seen white-tailed deer. Hell, I've seen red deer. But never a black one."

"We need to fortify ourselves. I do not know who they are or how many there will be, but we must hold out until morning. Does this place have a panic room?"

"Afraid not. From what I gathered, the lodge was built

in the seventies by the boy's grandfather after inheriting the family's railroad in Redbreast. Guess he got tired of laying his head among the common folk when visiting and wanted a place that offered more privacy. Anyway, as the years went on, he came here less and less. I think this place became more of a retreat for fishing and hunting than anything else. A panic room was never in the cards." Reginald said, moving to the door.

"Where are you going?"

"To check the circuit breaker. Like you said, darkness isn't the problem. It's what's in the dark that worries me. I want to see who I'm killing."

"Do not bother," Seko said. "Trust me. The power outage is no accident."

Thunder rumbled, vibrating the walls and surrounding windows.

REGINALD COLLECTED HIS hunting rifle from the kitchen, and despite Seko's discouraging words, he checked the circuit breaker anyhow. She had been right. Resetting the breaker did nothing to restore power to the house. In his frustration, he had slammed the circuit box shut, the force of which tore the door off its hinges.

Luckily for them, Alan kept kerosene lanterns on the property. Reginald used a couple to light August's bedroom, deciding it the best place to make their stand. He assured Seko the lodge's only conventional entrances were through the attached garage, kitchen patio, and front door. If anyone did decide to make a go at the bedroom's balcony, it would be like shooting fish in a barrel. The hallway was also in their favor. The floorboards were in dire need of replacing as the slightest amount of pressure made them whine.

"You must really care for the boy." Seko said.

Reginald finished adjusting the blankets taken from the bed and laid August onto the soft pallet. "Not always. When I first started this job, I said I'd give it six months. Six months became a year. A year became two years. Now here I am a decade later."

"Why did you stay?"

He joined her on the floor. They sat with their backs to the wall opposite the French doors leading to the balcony. Because the lodge sat empty for spans at a time, the doors were without drapes. "I don't know. I thought I'd be looking after some rotten to the core brat. He's not like that, though. Never has been. Sheltered for sure, but that's to be expected when parents hold on too tight."

Seko held the stuffed white rabbit in her lap. It must've fallen to the floor when Reginald removed the bed covers. "So you stayed because he is a good kid? Seems hardly a reason." She said.

He considered her question as he began loading the '76 Winchester with 40-60 two-hundred and sixty-grain ammunition. "You play a fly on the wall long enough you become one. People tend to forget you're there or nearby. They say and do all matter of things. Robert has it in his head that his wife's a *nigger*. Blames her for why Master August turned out the way he did."

Seko scoffed but said nothing.

"The misses is no angel herself. A real scorpion, that one. The things she says to her son."

"Then the boy must be glad to have you. Maybe you are here because you are supposed to be."

"I'm here because I choose to. His birthday's right around the corner, for crying out loud, and they decide to send him here while they sort their shit. I don't have the heart to tell him divorce is likely around the corner. If not for his grandfather suggesting the hunt, I probably would've already spilled the beans. I admit I had my reservations about taking him into the woods. But seeing him get that kill, seeing his face afterward, was well worth it." Reginald studied the woman's profile. "What about you, Ms. Seko? How does one become a little black bird?"

She sat the rabbit aside. Illuminated by the lantern's soft glow, the critter's red eyes appeared to glare at her. "One is born into the life. She then must earn the right to fly." She said and would have gone on if not for the manservant shushing her.

Gripping the rifle with both hands, Reginald's attention snapped to the balcony doors. They waited in silence. Beyond the doors' naked glass stood darkness so thick and pitch-black that he swore if he stepped outside, he would be able to feel it crawling all over him. There were no stars in the sky. No moon. Or perhaps the moon was hidden behind dense clouds laden with snow. The thought alone reminded Reginald of the coming storm and just how isolated they were from the rest of the world.

He turned the nearest lantern's knob counterclockwise, lowering the wick until he and Seko were cloaked almost entirely in shadow. The secondary lantern continued to burn. August's pale face remained visible as he lay slumbering on his back.

"Is there a way you can contact your organization?" Reginald asked.

"There was," Seko said. "The pendant can be used as a distress beacon. Whatever magical essence it had left, I gave to the boy. He can at least rest peacefully for a while."

"So it's just us then."

"Just us," Seko confirmed. "The good news is when an agent goes missing, the agency comes looking."

"I'll take whatever silver lining I can get."

"Can I ask you something?"

"Ms. Seko, I believe you just did. But I'm listening." Reginald spoke in a dry, focused tone. One he hadn't used in years. A tone from a time when he had worn the Huntsmen insignia on his shoulder and Crispin, known as Firefly in those days, couldn't go ten seconds without opening his mouth.

"Why are you going along with all of this?"

"I've told you. Can't deny what my eyes saw. I'm not fool enough to believe I know everything. Today I've seen things I've only ever read about in fairy tales. Things that shouldn't exist, yet here we are."

"I get that. But it does not really answer the question."

"I'm not sure I follow."

"When you spoke about the golem you faced, there was no trace of fear on you. In your eyes, I saw only sadness."

Reginald cast his gaze to the pallet watching the lantern's undulating light dance across his ward's face. "Twenty-seven years ago, I was on mission in Iraq. Some charges we set detonated prematurely, and because of that, I nearly missed extraction. In my haste to get out of there, I got spooked and blindly fired off a round. Before I knew what had happened, it was already too late." He paused, wetting his lips before continuing. "There was this kid standing right in front of me. He asked me something. He asked if I was death. It was dark, and there was fire spreading all over the place. When I looked at that kid, I saw the top of his head was gone. I knew I had done that. All I could do was watch as that boy's body caught up with what was left of his brain. Then I left."

He half expected Seko to say something. When she didn't, he figured there was nothing to say. No words that could make his crooked straight. "But that isn't the worst of it. When I left Iraq, I left behind the memory of that boy. Today, twenty-seven years later, it all came rushing back. It was like someone dug a hook into my brain and was pulling everything to the surface."

"Weaving," Seko said, racking the SIG pistol. "It is called weaving. People who can do this are rare in the world. The good ones plant calming thoughts and dreams into the minds of the sick and dying. The bad ones attack the minds of their victims. Haunts them with their own memories."

"How does one fight against something like that?" Reginald asked.

"I will keep an eye on you best I can. Just know the boy comes first."

"Naturally."

"And thank you for sharing that information with me."

"Just the ramblings of an old man forced to revisit his past misdeeds."

"Well, because of those ramblings, I now know our enemy is at least two."

"How do you figure?"

"Nowhere has the veil ever granted any person more than one gift."

Reginald needed no further explanation. Outside, the wind stirred, rattling the balcony doors. The glass itself began to crystalize with frost, and lightning crackled across the sky. For less than a second, he saw the heavy snowfall. It fell in sheets gusting straight at the house, a stark contradiction of what the morning forecast had predicted. The manservant knew if the storm kept this pace, they would be in for a complete whiteout.

Knowing this is not what urged him to lean his back off the wall or the reason behind why he strained his eyes to see through the frosting glass. He thought he had seen something. Seko must have also seen it because she mimicked his alert posture.

"Did you see that?" Reginald queried.

"I did," Seko said.

No sooner than the words left her mouth did one of the floorboards directly outside the bedroom door creak. Seko bolted up onto one knee with the pistol at the ready and had done so without making a sound. Reginald heard it too but kept his gaze on the glass doors hoping for another lightning strike. None came. Instead, the sound of gusting wind grew into a bestial snarl that rattled the doors with tremendous force. A wind so cold the ice overtook the glass in a matter of seconds. He reinforced his grip on the rifle as the ice splintered and cracked in the face of the unrelenting wind.

They were in the thick of it now. This bastard storm that manifested so quickly and abruptly he hoped that its presence had taken their enemy with equal, if not greater, surprise. Then it happened. The lightning he had been waiting for struck so close to the house the walls shook. The entire room flashed white. He hadn't heard the glass shatter but felt cuts open on the back of his hands and face, prompting him to shield himself with an arm while squeezing his eyes shut.

He sneered as the frigid wind tore through the room, but before the thought even entered his mind to fight against it, it was gone. The lights of the lanterns, too, were snuffed out. Beyond the shattered glass doors, Reginald could hear the sound of electricity crackling and thought by some miracle power was restored to the house, and perhaps a line on the property had fallen. Opening his eyes, he saw he was mistaken.

Beside the pallet knelt a person looking down at his sleeping charge. A boy who appeared to be about the same age as August, but that is where their similarities ended. For Michigan weather, the boy was severely underdressed. That is if wearing a leather loincloth could be considered dressing at all. His skin was darker than dark and covered in indistinguishable markings.

The reason why Reginald could make them out to some degree was for the same reason he couldn't bring himself to move a muscle. Electricity leaped off the boy, who seemed to have manifested out of thin air. Snake-like tendrils of pure energy buzzed and crackled as they streaked across the wooden floorboards in every direction. Reginald knew then what his ears had heard, and his heart was pounding so hard in his chest he felt if he so much as twitched, he'd kill over. The instinctual gut feeling of fight or flight plunged his mind into a lake of despair. However, the choice was made for him the second the entity moved to take August from the blankets.

"Don't do it!" Seko shouted. Her words of warning meant nothing to the manservant. On his feet, he took aim with the rifle and squeezed the lever tight. For the first time, he saw the entity's eyes and in them raged a thunderstorm. Everything happened so fast: His finger on the trigger. The heat through his chest. The pain and violent muscle spasms.

Reginald barely comprehended the bolt of lightning striking him, nor did he recall crashing into the wall at his back despite the evidence of impact. What he did know with absolute certainty was that he was on the floor. He did not need to look at the pallet to know it was empty. Through blurred vision, he saw Seko take cover near the balcony as a bolt of lightning obliterated the wooden balustrade. He saw it outlined against the night sky, not a humanoid figure but a winged being of prehistoric proportion. This time he did not freeze. Numb, tingling hands wrestled the rifle off the floor, and he aimed at the pitch-black.

"Come on," Reginald growled, his words slurred and sweat stinging his eyes. "Come on," he repeated, wiping the sweat from his brow and readjusting the rifle in his clammy hands. His eyes stayed the darkness. Didn't blink. Couldn't risk it. If he did believe in God, he supposed now was good a time as any to ask for a miracle. Not for himself but for young August, who deserved it.

He didn't get the chance to ask. Like spider webs, lightning streaked across the sky with a long and unearthly reach. Reginald's eyes drunk in every ounce of available light and saw the beat of enormous grey-silver wings in the distance. *Seventy yards*, he thought. He took aim. Not where the creature was at but where he knew it would be. He pulled the trigger.

The rifle sounded off with a resounding boom. Seko balked. Beyond the smoldering balustrade, an agonizing screech rang out, followed by a distinct metallic crash. Both sounds told Reginald most of what he needed to know. He scooped a lantern in hand and shuffled it and the rifle to his offhand long enough to find his lighter. Once he restored fire to the wick, he grabbed the bedroom doorknob.

"Wait. You cannot just go out there." Seko said.

Reginald turned to her, glaring. "For all I know, I just killed him."

CHAPTER 16

REGINALD EJECTED THE SPENT CARTRIDGE from the rifle. It somersaulted in the air before clattering to the floor and rolling beneath the bedroom door. The door opened with a groan. Seko entered the hallway first, clearing the corners with pistol in one hand and the lantern in the other. When she signaled the OK, Reginald followed. She had convinced him to slow down, to use the thing in his head called a brain. He agreed, albeit begrudgingly.

Together the pair made their way down the long corridor. To Reginald, it felt endless. For the first time, he wondered just why in the hell did any person need a house this damned big. During the day, the halls were warm and inviting, and the window at the opposite end ushered in an abundance of sunlight. At night the chandelier overhead along with the electric wall lamps, reminiscent of thirteenth-century candlesticks and holders, kept the lodge's inviting nature intact. With those things gone, the lodge had become a frigid shell.

The kerosene lantern disrupted the corridor's perfect symmetry in a show of bouncing light and deeply carved shadows. Walls that earlier in the day appeared, at best, a decade old now looked to have aged by no less than a century. Reginald felt like an unwelcomed prowler in an unfamiliar place.

Most modern families hang pictures in their homes for no reason other than to make the statement that says *We were here*. Something to be glanced at in passing by the young and offer a feel-good reminder to empty nesters of a time they can never get back. For all the differences in the world, the family photo is universally commonplace in developed nations. There are plenty of homes decorated by matching sweater clans, graduating sons and daughters, and dear old dad when he had hair on his head. Each photograph a little time capsule in and of itself.

There is one more thing the majority of these people have in common. Once they shuffle off this mortal coil, history won't bat an eye. The same could not be said for members of the Foxx clan. The black and white photographs occupying the corridor told the story of a time long past but still very much relevant today.

In 1901 at age twenty-one, Alexander Foxx is at a ribbon-cutting ceremony in Redbreast, Michigan, to celebrate the opening of the Braeden Railroad. To his left stands then-mayor

RUN RABBIT RUN

Henry Oldman, and to his right, his business associate, a black man named Abraham Samson I, whose family is the second-largest supplier of salt in the US. The mayor is grinning big like he'd hit the Megalodon Jackpot while neither Alexander nor Abraham crack so much as a smile.

The average twenty-one-year-old waits for nightfall before venturing out on weekends. They have to go out and do so in packs, eager to spend the earnings of their meager wages. Because at twenty-one, it is their legal obligation to suck down as much booze as humanly possible. They can do it loudly and proudly without fear of reprimand. Come morning they will hate themselves only to do it all over again. This is their inheritance, their tradition. And while some of them may go on to live productive lives, again, history will not remember them.

In the second photograph, Alexander cuts the ribbon. The camera's shutter closes and opens at the right moment, forever capturing the severed ends wavy flight. Onlookers are in mid-applause. Henry Oldman and Abraham Samson I smile.

The third photograph is the real showstopper. An engineering marvel that set the Braeden Company apart from its competitors. Designed and assembled in 1900, the locomotive was built specifically with the landmark occasion in mind. An up-close and personal full-frontal showcases the unique curves and rivet pattern of the menacing black steel that makes the engine look futuristic even by today's standards.

In the first month of operation, the locomotive transported more than ten thousand tons of rock salt along the shortline rail. Alexander, who had been a traditionalist and respected his predecessors, named the engine thirty-six, after the thirty-six empowerment laws on which his family's house was built. To further emphasize his commitment to lineage, the locomotive's number plate read eighteen, eighteen.

Reginald did not see legacy on the walls or the proud accomplishments achieved by captains of industry. What he saw was phantoms haunting a cold hallway in a place that had become more house than home in a matter of hours. Luther Vandross came to mind. *A room is still a room, even when there's nothin' there but gloom.*

"Do you want to know? You should." Seko said.

Reginald nearly missed her words altogether. Thoughts about his mother swam in his head. He could see her face, tight and tired. She had been against him running off to join the *white man's military*, insisting on numerous occasions they had their own war to fight. She had spoken the truth, and he had seen it with his own eyes in '81 at age thirteen. The coppers, the screams, the way Brixton burned. But it was the war within the four walls of their home that terrified him above any other.

His father had been a one-man army of cruel fury who tore through their flat in a whirlwind of curses, blows, and meanness for no other reason than just cause. Back then, Reginald had believed in prayer and spent many nights on his knees with hands clasped, pleading to the bearded man in the clouds to deliver his mother and brother from his father's tyranny. He was the eldest, the biggest, and therefore had offered to take the brunt of his father's storm.

RUN RABBIT RUN

Despite Reginald's hopes and prayers, things had gone from bad to worse when the man lost his job. Not only had the man's work put food on the table and a roof over their heads, but him leaving the flat each day was a ceasefire for them. A glance at normality and a chance to experience sanity for a short while.

Reginald recalled taking full advantage of his father's absence. He remembered the way he and his brother begged their mother to take them away and how she, a woman who stepped out of her parent's home and straight into marriage, had refused. He had called her a coward. She had slapped him and instantly regretted it.

He recalled making up his mind then and there. He was sixteen, stuffing some clothes and *all* of his anger in a bag. He set out for the *white man's military* while his father hurled curses at his back. *You aren't worth the salt on the table.* He could hear the words ringing in his ears. That had been the last time he saw his father.

"What does it matter?" The words oozed from Reginald's mouth like molasses. He did not know whether he was speaking to himself or responding to the question asked. What was the question? Right. Seko expected him to ask the obvious. To want to know what the thing was that attacked them and stole August away.

He concluded it didn't matter. Whatever it was wasn't impervious to bullets, and therefore could be killed. He was good at killing. Had made a career out of taking lives. He thought about legacy now. His legacy as they continued along the corridor under the watchful ghoulish gaze of generational wealth.

"It matters," Seko said. "It matters because something like that does not belong here. Impundulu does not belong here. Hey. Are you listening? Are you all right?"

Reginald made no answer.

Seko stopped walking, and he bumped against her, nearly knocking her over with the strength of a lumbering ox. "I knew it. You are in shock. I am surprised impundulu's bolt did not strike you dead."

Her mouth was moving, but her words sounded muffled as he passed her by. Then he heard it.

"Are you death?" The words seeped between his ears. Although Reginald hadn't spoken the Arabic tongue in decades, he recognized it straight away. Above all, he knew who spoke them and understood their meaning. He felt like his legs were suddenly encased in bronze, each one weighing a ton apiece, rooting him in place.

Seko came alongside him, bringing the light. "You need to stop. Killing yourself before we even reach the front door is not going to help anyone. Open your shirt. Let me see if your bandages have come undone."

Reginald did not comply. His eyes stared straight ahead at the darkened staircase about twenty feet from where they were. He could see light in the stairwell. Faint at first, but its potency steadily grew in shades of yellow and orange. "You don't see that?"

"See what?" Seko glanced back over her shoulder. "There is nothing to see."

He knew that was a lie. It had to be. How could Seko not see it? It was right there. Even if he chose to believe she did not see the growing light rising in the stairwell, there was no way she could miss the smokey smell or heat wafting at them.

Reginald squeezed the rifle so tightly his hands went numb. Sweat made his shirt cling to him. With eyes wide, he witnessed the impossible for the third time tonight. The old saying about bad things happening in threes came to mind. Maybe it wasn't bad. Maybe it was the universe catching up with him for all the bad things he had done. Sure he did not subscribe to such silly superstitions, but seeing was believing. What he saw was nightmarish.

A small fiery foot climbed the final stair. Each step taken left smoldering brimstone in its wake. Where there should have been brain matter and skull fragments within the thing's cratered head, a fiery cauldron blazed. Beneath the cauldron was the Baghdadi boy's half-charred face. There he stood wearing the same hospital gown worn on that fateful night. However, the gown was tattered and weighted with black soot.

"Are you death?" The ghoul repeated the question. Having no lips, the words filtered through exposed teeth and burnt sinew jaw muscles. His voice was raw calluses and his eyes the colorless grey of the dead.

"It was an accident," Reginald said. The big man wrung his hands around the rifle then dropped it altogether. The weapon thudded against the hardwood floor. "No one was supposed to be there. The entire floor was on lockdown. Why didn't you just stay in your room? Why didn't you die there like the rest of them?" His voice trembled. A far cry from the authoritative baritone capable of putting a lion to shame.

It was one thing to kill a child armed with a machine

gun, but to murder unarmed civilians was wicked to the core. Not once had Reginald carried out such a barbaric order. "You think *I'm* death? You're death. Your government is death. *My* government is death. You think they gave a damn about you? You think they give a shit? I've got news for you. We're all just walking statistics on borrowed time, and God's not the one out here punching people's tickets. Oh no, man can do bad all by himself and has been doing bad since the dawn of time."

"Are you death?" The ghoul nagged, taking a step forward.

Reginald's face was a combination of perspiration, tears, and mucus. "I'm what they shaped me to be." He pleaded. His lips quivered, glistening with spittle. "Aren't you listening? Haven't you heard a word I've said? I didn't know any better. It's what they do to you when you're young. They take all that anger, all that pain, and unleash you onto the world. Promise to make a man out of you. What they don't tell you is that when all the anger's gone, all that's left is the guilt, the emptiness, and the real world where no one can relate. A world where your own mother can't even look you in the face. A world where each day you have to convince yourself you aren't a monster."

The boy... The thing that used to be a boy opened its mouth wide. Its jaws creaked, stretched beyond human limitation. The sinew muscles pulled so taut they snapped like dry, cracked rubber, and bottom jaw flopped forward in a grotesque display of teeth and tongue. Deep within the depths of the thing's bowels emanated an inhuman roar, and without warning, it charged.

Reginald threw up his hands and screamed.

CHAPTER 17

SEKO WAS MOMENTARILY DUMBSTRUCK BY the butler's outburst. She thought for certain the man was experiencing a psychotic break. She should have expected as much. The world, as the butler knew it, had been flipped on its head.

She hated the situation. Her simple reconnaissance mission turned royal clusterfuck. She had no one other than herself to blame for the series of bad decisions made thus far. She should have died in the snow. In an act of cowardice—or so she told herself—she activated the pendant's synthesized veil essence to sustain her life and repair the damage done to her body.

On the flip side, there was a part of Seko that believed if she trusted in the beacon, all would have been lost. August would have fallen into the hands of the veil-touched sooner, and she would have died a meaningless death.

She was wet behind the ears. Metaphorically pushed out the nest as a test to prove herself worthy enough to advance to the next level. It was supposed to be simple; scout, report and keep the boy safe. Nothing more, nothing less.

"A world where each day you have to convince yourself you aren't a monster." The butler blubbered.

"Stop it!" Seko chided in a futile attempt to keep her voice at a whisper. If someone were lurking in the lodge waiting to ambush them, then the manservant's wild outburst had no doubt given away their position. "There is nothing there. Remember what I told you. They are weaving on you. Planting lies in your head!"

Seko hoped that her words could convince him. That by some chance, they could breach the illusion and bring him back to reality. But if her words did fail, she was prepared to do the necessary. In the butler's right state of mind, she knew she could handle him just fine. As he was now, her gut told her death was the only viable response if he were to attack.

She rested her finger on the pistol's trigger.

While Magpie did not deem it necessary to concern themselves with the help's well-being, Seko saw value in keeping the butler alive. He may have been an old man, but he wasn't a decrepit old man. An old soldier, at that. To be blunt, she needed him. Because she had only a vague idea when it came to what they were up against, and two was better than one.

The butler cried out. Before he had, Seko thought she heard something else. A creaking sound that had barely been there at all. Steadfast, she spun on her heels and raised the lantern. Its brilliant light wavered, becoming muted by the darkness that lay ahead.

Something was there. Many somethings Seko's brain couldn't rightly identify. One after another—occasionally in unison—they glowed a pulsing seductive green reminding her of fireflies during summer nights. Then she thought about stars pressed against the black void of space.

The tiny beacons blinking their peculiar and unrecognizable Morse code started at the floor and reached for the high ceiling overhead. By the time Seko put the pieces together, the ground was already shaking beneath her. It was at that moment the butler screamed as something thundered down the corridor with remarkable speed.

Seko raised the pistol and fired. The SIG Sau reported three times. The muzzle erupted in miniature fireballs lasting for less than a second apiece. For her, it was enough to confirm she hadn't been the only one brought back to life. In a blur, she glimpsed charred wood, smoldering orange embers, and compacted white ash. A testament to the destructive force her incendiary grenade had unleashed on the golem.

The colossus's entire left side was in ruin. The creature's right side was healthy interwoven vines and a thick birch exoskeleton housing a matrix of fluorescent plant life.

The second it had taken for Seko to process this information took the humanoid behemoth less to close the distance between them. The three shots fired did nothing to slow the colossus's pace, and in one sweeping motion, she was swatted aside with the same cold indifference as one would a fly. Her teeth rattled in her skull when she slammed against a sturdy door. The hinges buckled but held, and her body rag-dolled to the floor for the brief instance her soul departed her flesh.

Her eyes shot open. Seko realized the behemoth had gone straight through her to the butler. She could hear their chaotic and brutal exchange unfolding in the dark. Intuition told her the old man didn't have the upper hand.

She groaned, forced herself to sit up. A couple of feet from her was the lantern on its side, the wick continuing to carry a flame. She outstretched her fingers, curled them around the pistol, which was nearest. She next reached for the lantern, stopped.

Seko bounced to her feet in a crouch and pressed herself tight to the door at her back. No sooner than she did, a red beam cut a path across where her hand had been, and the corridor erupted in gunfire. Nine shots rang out in three consecutive bursts per trigger pull.

"Ahh!" Seko shrieked as the ninth round punched through her right thigh. The insurmountable pain nearly rendered her immobile right then and there, but her training told her she needed to either move or die.

Reaching behind her, she fumbled for the door's lever. Found it. Seko pulled the lever down, throwing herself back hard as she could, and hoped the fucking door was unlocked. It was. She spilled into the room onto her back, drenched in sweat and panting like an insane person. Her leg felt like it was on fire.

Muscle memory kicked in. Seko bolted upright, blind firing through the wall in the direction the initial shots had come. She did so to buy herself some time. She fired two shots, paused, fired another two, paused again. The third time after shooting, she used her heels to propel herself across the floor, not stopping until she was out of the doorway's line of sight.

Within seconds a silhouette appeared in the door. The cloaked figure dropped to one knee. A red laser sight cut a wide swath across the room from end to end as the person went about clearing the corners. Satisfied, they stepped fully inside the room and Seko was tempted to spring from where she hid.

She convinced herself to stay put. It was a good thing she had. Whomever this intruder was who no doubt was aiding the veil-touched, if not veil-touched themselves, switched on a tactical flashlight. The shadows retreated.

REGINALD'S EYES DRANK deep the sight of churning fire and brimstone. Pungent sulfur vapors overpowered his nostrils, and his ears filled with ghostly cries trapped in an eternal loop of damnation. He could hear the bombs, the gunfire, the anguish and dismay expressed in a rainbow of languages. All of these things originated in the ghoulish boy's fiery throat as if it were a hellish gateway linked to the manservant's past. In a boom, it was all gone.

His consciousness struggled to surface as if it had been dragged down to the ocean floor and left to drown. When his eyes did open, he saw vibrant green dots floating in darkness. Pain ricocheted along his spinal cord, telling him what he needed to know about the boom. It would seem that sturdy timber walls don't give beneath flesh and bone. His feet weren't touching the ground.

Around his throat, something seized him, choked him, wanted to break him. But he was not a man easily broken. He grabbed the grabber. What he felt gave him pause. Where there should have been flesh, he found none. Seko's cautionary words came rushing back. *The golem I encountered, I think, was meant for you*, she had said.

Reginald's head tilted back, gazed up at the one looming two feet above his. The face looking down was no man's. No ghoul's. An ashen oval creation, hard tree bark and deeply grooved. Boney spikes, white at the roots and black at the tips, protruded from its flat forehead forming a half halo. Its eyes were burning verdelite: haunting, primordial, and deceptively beautiful. The woods come to life.

He glanced down and saw the luminous green dots clearly. They blinked a steady rhythm, embedded within intricate winding vines encased behind an impregnable skeletal chassis. They were like neurons firing, crisscrossing to and fro.

Freed from the weave that entangled his mind, Reginald drove his fists into the colossus's chest. He used the wall as leverage to put real power behind each blow. He landed punch after punch. Each punch landed stripped the skin from his knuckles and blood made his fingers sticky. Regardless, he could not stop. He would not stop until he burst a hole through the creature's chest. The colossus had other plans.

He was lifted higher in the air, so high his blows no longer connected. The colossus's elongated arm extended to its full length then drove him straight into the ground. His head bounced off the floorboards, sweat and blood splatter left in its wake. Before he could process what happened, he was plucked up again and flung at the wall. He made a sound he hadn't heard himself make before and as he crashed to the floor, glass from broken picture frames rained down on him.

Reginald laid unmoving for a long while. Had he heard gunfire? Or maybe more echoes of his past calling, and it was time for him to answer. He saw his mother's, brother's, and August's faces. He thought about legacy. What legacy would he leave behind? Perhaps some mixed breed child or children who did not know he existed. While they teetered on an identity tightrope in a country where it was commonplace to run around barefoot in the mud, he had lived a life of convenience.

Were they outcasts cursed to be called roach or monkey because of his seed? Would they lie down with tourists just to put food on the table? He knew because he had seen such things. He thought about August again. Would the boy die as a result of him dying? Then Reginald stopped thinking and stopped seeing.

LIKE A DEER in headlights, Seko, froze and the rifle let loose again. In three consecutive bursts per trigger pull, bullets punched through the exposed antique wood frame of the tall bed adjacent the door. The elegant illustration carved in the bed's side rail depicted a thirteenth-century hunting party. The party's huntsmen and porters all knelt with their faces pressed to the earth while their king held a sickly child in his arms. He looked to be pleading with a tall eighteen-point buck.

In a matter of seconds, the beautiful craftsmanship was gone, reduced to sawdust. The mattress itself a hole-filled heap of exposed springs.

Seko knew she would have done the same had their roles been reversed. Hiding under the bed was the obvious choice for a frightened person uninitiated to the game of life and death. She held her breath. No, not because she was afraid. She needed to calm down, control her breathing, and not draw attention to herself now that the gunfire had ceased.

The rifle's tactical flashlight swept over the room. Its blinding artificial dawn brought life to critters long deceased. Alan Foxx's master suite was a trophy hunter's wet dream and a housekeeper's worst nightmare. Glinting taxidermy owls, wolves, and bison eyes stared at the masked intruder with frozen territorial glares. A falcon perched on the highest point the room had to offer—with its beak agape and wings spread— screeched in perpetual silence.

Seko listened to the heavy footfalls approach and felt gratitude for the attire given to her. The black athletic gear helped her blend in with the family of black bears (a mother and its two cubs) as she pressed herself flat to mama bear's back and waited.

"You're quite the resilient little bird, aren't you? We thought for sure you died. No pulse. With your insides spilling to the outside. But it would seem that your kind is just full of surprises. Are you veil-touched? No, that can't be it. We would have sensed it in you." The intruder said. A woman's voice. Sweet like candy. Foreign.

Seko did not take the bait. Unlike in the movies, shooting a gun wildly in a room with limited visibility in hopes of hitting one's target was foolish. Not only that, but guns did not have unlimited bullets in a magazine. It was for that reason she was being stalked. The intruder could either be a professional or a novice but what they weren't was a complete imbecile.

She wished she had at least gotten a glance at the rifle. That way, she could have made an educated guess of its magazine compacity and use the information to launch a proper counterattack. No matter. With or without the knowledge, and time a precious commodity she could no longer afford to spare, she needed to make a decision fast.

"How did you do it?" The intruder pressed. Footfalls drew closer to the ensemble of immortalized trophies. The tactical flashlight penetrated the red wolf pack, locked in a battle of fangs and fury. The gleam in their amber eyes told a different truth. "Let me guess… A trinket of some kind? Your organization is shrouded in mystery, but bit by bit, we chip away at your secrets. The only logical conclusion is that Magpie has alchemists in its ranks. Good to know."

The rifle and its flashlight trained on the massive bison pair. Seko could feel the net tightening around her just as much as she could feel her right leg throbbing. Adrenaline gave her the shakes and she knew it was now or never. At the start of this game of cat and mouse, she half-expected the intruder to check the balcony, storm the master bath, or tear apart the wardrobe searching for her. But no, erratic behavior like that was carried out by someone who was either nervous, desperate, or both. The masked bitch was cool as a cucumber.

It did not take long for Seko to understand what this was. A cleanup job. They had what they wanted and were tying up loose ends. She could hear the intruder move away from the bison. Like a bloodhound, footsteps were closing in on her position. She put together why and her chest tightened. Gunshot wound. Blood trail. Flashlight.

In sync with the intruder's steps, she shouldered mama bear to test the old girl's weight. Standing on hind legs, mama bear was over six feet tall. She did not rock, but Seko did detect some give. The intruder stopped, and because she had, the opportunity to test again was out of the question.

A sun bear stared dead-eyed at the glaring light beam. Seko knew she, mama bear, and the cubs were next in line. She flexed her round shoulders. Using her left leg for stability, she threw herself hard as she could into mama bear's back with a bang. The rifle snapped up in her direction, the flashlight blinding. She squeezed her eyes shut and continued to push. The rifle's muzzle ignited with bright flashes as a single trigger pull put three holes in mama bear's stomach.

By no means did the bullets stop mama from teetering forward. But for a split second, Seko thought teetering is all the bear would do.

The intruder let out a startled cry flinging herself aside. She scarcely avoided being crushed beneath fur, teeth, and claws. Even so, there was no putting on the brakes for what was already in motion.

Seko ducked behind one of the cubs. She raised the pistol, aimed in the direction where she saw the flashlight bouncing sporadically, and opened fire. The mother bear continued its predetermined path, parting the male and female Blakiston's fish owls, shoving aside a massive bison, and crashing through the red wolf pack, all to get at the intruder. Although she fell short, mama bear had served her purpose. A thick dust cloud permeated the room. The SIG Sauer's magazine had run dry, and that meant it was time to move.

"You bitch!" The intruder screeched, her sweetness gone. She pointed the rifle in one direction, fired. Pointed it in another, fired again. The tactical flashlight was as useful as a pair of high beams in a thick fog.

Seko took flight, soared, her feet not making a sound. She cut a wide path to close the distance between her and the intruder, using the muffled flashlight as a marker. Before colliding, her hand traveled to her back, drew the white-handled knife sheathed there. Her dominant hand thrust forward with the accuracy of a skilled swordsman. Her left firmly grabbed the rifle and pushed it out and away from her.

The blade connected, blunted hard against the hidden bulletproof vest the intruder wore. The average wrist would have shattered on impact. Seko recalculated, knew what she needed to do. Draw the knife back, flip it to an inverted grip, and go for the vulnerable sweet spot, where the vest ends and the flesh begins.

The mind was always faster than the body. In truth, she should have been thinking and doing at the same time. As a result of not doing, Seko's face tingled with stinging annoyance. The masked bitch had punched her: a clean left hook square across the jaw that told her right then and there this person was no fighter.

When the second punch came, Seko accepted its arrival. Her hand repositioned on the knife. She came up, over and under the extended arm, burying the blade between the woman's ribs.

Behind the mask, the intruder wheezed in a mixture of shock and pain.

Seko kept her lesser hand on the rifle. In one motion, she swept the intruder's legs from under her. Together they fell to the floor. Light from the waning crescent moon spilled in through the balcony doors. It flickered in and out as if someone were playing with a dimmer switch. However, the storm was responsible: a heavy whiteout with snowflakes the size of silver dollars.

She grimaced. Her teeth clenched to suppress a scream. The intruder squirmed under her, groped, and found the wound in her right thigh. Fingers dug in, twisting, shoving, pulling, and raking like a wild animal. Tears blurred her vision, and impulse told her to let the rifle go.

The gun barked and kicked against the dusty hardwood floor. Bullets flew, busting up an antique chifforobe. Seko scrambled to find the knife jutting from the intruder's side. When she did, she twisted it.

The intruder howled but kept squeezing the trigger.

Not once. Not twice. But when Seko slammed the intruder's wrist to the floor the third time, wood cracked bone, and the rifle stopped. She shoved it away.

"Where is the boy?" She panted. "Where is August Foxx?"

Grey-green eyes peered at her from behind the mask. Whoever designed the face-covering had done so painstakingly. The lips were stained black. Around the eyes, too, in thick swan-shaped brush strokes. Stars crowned her forehead, three on either side of a crescent moon that mirrored the sky.

"Say something." Seko forced the knife deeper.

The intruder writhed. "You should go home, little bird. Fly away from this place."

"Tell me what I want to know, witch. Where did impundulu take the boy? I know about the demon deer you worship. The one you call the Pale King."

"You're a young fool." The intruder said.

Then Seko felt it. A push. A kind of pressure building inside her head. The pressure filled her so completely she thought she was having an aneurysm. She felt nauseated. Blood trickled from her nose and ran down over her lips. When the red droplets splotched the white mask below, it rippled like water then disappeared.

She was transported to a white room surrounded by black girls no older than ten. They danced elegantly, wearing black leotards and matching tutus. She saw herself and tensed. Tall, bulky, and uncoordinated, Seko had been nothing like her peers.

She missed several steps before being reprimanded. A woman much taller than her approached. Rod in hand, she struck the young Seko on the upper thigh. A second blow bruised her knuckles, and long fingers gripped the barre tight.

"This is not real," Seko told herself, frowning. "That bitch is messing around in my head." Perhaps the intent had been to weaken her. To show her something traumatic as was done with the butler to prey upon his inner demons.

While the road to becoming a Magpie was paved in tedious trials and tribulations, Seko never felt ostracized for her shortcomings. Her sisters embraced her. They rose together. In other words, what the witch showed her only served to piss her off.

She shut her eyes, taking a deep breath. She drew her head back, paused, then rammed it forward and down. Her past shattered like glass. Hundreds of pieces danced, twirled, and twinkled, showing multiple black-clad arms waving and kicking in unison. Then the present emerged in perfect clarity.

Seko sat astride the intruder, hand gripping the knife. Her head pounded as she glared down at the mask she had split in two. She brushed the two halves aside and beheld a face that was neither young nor old. Deep-set grey-green eyes stared, unblinking. The skin was a bruised bluish tint, paper-thin with a crushed and bloodied nose that had retreated inside the skull. "No more tricks, witch. Where is the boy?"

"They took everything from us." The intruder wheezed. "They'll take what's yours too."

"How many of you are there?"

"It matters not. The boy is no longer of any consequence to you. By his blood, we will be restored to our former glory. The Light will see us through." As if resigned to her fate, the intruder turned her face towards the snowfall.

Understanding that she would get no meaningful answers, Seko pulled the knife free. The intruder winced but didn't make a sound. She hesitated a moment then slit the emaciated husk's throat. *The veil takes its toll*, she thought, watching with morbid curiosity as the lifeblood left the witch's body.

After the gurgling ceased, she checked for trinkets so as not to make the same mistake they had about her.

I'm GOING TO *die here*, Reginald thought. His left eye was sealed shut. It was only a matter of time. He had run out of steam avoiding the colossus's attacks. The golem was swift in a straight line, but in close quarters it lumbered using wide-sweeping strikes. For this reason, he continued to draw breath.

He attempted to get around the colossus to no avail, tried to escape through the open doorway where he and Seko had taken their brief refuge. The problem with that plan was the creature's wide girth. It must've been two if not three times wider than himself. He was cornered.

Reginald kept his guard up. He stole glances at the open doorway as if expecting by some bizarre phenomenon he would teleport to it. Stranger things have happened. Tonight, especially. It called to him, mocked him, brightened in splashes of moonlight. So close, yet so far.

Like a javelin, the colossus drew back its arm. Wood and vines creaked and moaned, its fingers melding together, forming one gigantic spike. He watched, panting. Sweat beaded his forehead and dripped into his good eye. He could see the attack coming, telegraphed by ironically festive green lights that weren't lights and a bright palpitating red core. But his feet remained motionless, welded to the floor.

Reginald knew if he took a step in any direction, he would collapse. He chose to die standing. The javelin hurtled towards his chest with remarkable speed and time stretched its hand towards him. In its palm, he saw his mother, brother, and the Baghdadi boy whose cratered head was a stew of plasma and grey brain matter. *You aren't worth the salt on the table!* His father's words invaded the vortex of eternity like a foul wind.

Hand outstretched, he hadn't heard the glass break. The fire is what halted him.

The golem roared in anguish. Flames scurried along the behemoth's back, devouring bark and oxygen in greedy gulps.

Reginald's legs gave, and he fell on his backside, watching wide-eyed as the abomination staggered away. Its right arm flailed, smacking itself across the shoulders and back in desperation, and he felt mild relief when the elongated appendage set ablaze.

The colossus's bellowing roar dominated the lodge's interior, raising one octave after another before dying out in a shrill cry. What remained of the eight-foot-tall behemoth was a pyre engulfed in a raging inferno. Reginald thought the lodge was doomed to be swept up in the fire's hunger. Himself included. What followed was no less jarring but the preferred outcome.

The pyre toppled over, impacting the floor with a thud as it burst apart, scattering thousands of smoldering indistinguishable chunks in every direction. Seeing the creature undone, he could hardly believe the thing had ever been alive.

"Hey. Are you dead over there?" A voice called out to him. Right away, Reginald knew to whom it belonged. A high-powered flashlight flipped on. Seko appeared behind it. She limped, stepping over the colossus's smoldering remnants and crushing broken lantern glass underfoot.

"You know, I'm bloody well tired of this Lord of the Rings walking trees shit." Reginald said.

Seko paused, looked at him. Without a word, she drew a knife from behind her back.

Reginald's brows creased, concerned. He searched her face for answers and found none. Was her mind under attack? Were they weaving on her? He knew how fast it could be. One minute you're yourself, and the next, it's like an invisible hand squeezing the mind.

She turned from him, and his eyes followed. He saw it then: a black mass among fiery debris that had been death on two legs. Seko kicked it over. The black crust broke off in a spray of embers and soot, revealing a pulsating fleshy red cube underneath. Vines small enough to be mistaken for veins crisscrossed the thrumming thing.

"What in the hell is that?" Reginald heard himself say. He had a sinking feeling he knew. He stared at the smoking, gurgling cube, watched as it oozed a neon green fluid that brought a single word to mind: RADIOACTIVE.

"The heart," Seko said, confirming his suspicions. She stooped, plunged the knife into the glowing mass up to the hilt. Beyond the lodge's walls, what sounded like a wildcat yowled. The heart gurgled, sputtered, ejecting copious amounts of the mysterious ooze, and its color faded to no color at all. "Can you walk?"

"I could ask you the same." Reginald acknowledged the cloth tied around her upper thigh. "Thought I heard gunfire." The sight of the AUG assault rifle told him he had heard right.

"It is nothing. The bullet was only passing through."

He almost grinned at that. "And the gunman?"

"A veil-touched. I am sure she was the one screwing about inside your head."

"And where is she now?"

"Dead. I had no choice."

"What do you mean you didn't have a choice? Did she say anything about August? Is he alive? Anything about their numbers? And you just killed her without getting any information?"

"I could not get her to talk."

"I could have."

"Yes, you shot impundulu from the sky. But the boy is not dead. If so, the veil-touched would have said that much. Of this, I know."

"How can you be so sure?"

"They came here for one reason and one reason only. That reason is waiting for us. Waiting for you out there. They made the mistake of underestimating us and it cost them one of their own. I ask you again now. Can you walk?"

Reginald panted, still chasing his second wind. He weighed her words then nodded. "Yes, I think I can manage."

"Then get up. The night is not done, and neither are we." Seko extended a hand, and the manservant took it.

CHAPTER 18

AUGUST GROANS, SINKING IN THE soft blue beanbag chair with red polka dots. It holds him snug as a glove. He always preferred the multicolored beanbags over the firm cots when it came to naptime.

"Mrs. Davies, could you shut the window? It's a bit nippy." He mumbles. Unbeknownst to him, Mrs. Davies—who was pushing sixty when they first met during his primary school days—has been pushing up daisies going on four years now.

He cherishes these memories, which at the moment are far closer to reality than dream. They represent the best part of his life. A time before elves, undead minions, and girls invade his psyche. A time before the disease ravages his body and robs him of a proper childhood. A time before back-to-back doctor visits, grueling physical examinations, and experimental treatments that did more harm than good.

It may have sounded cynical to say coming out of the mouth of a boy who appeared to have everything, but by August's firsthand account, he had become more lab rat than child.

"How many times must I say it, August? If you want the window shut, then get up and shut it." Mrs. Davies said. She was not the type to yield to spoil children just because their mommies and daddies had a bit more heft to their bank accounts than she did. She had believed that responsibility and accountability were something to be groomed into a child as soon as they could walk and form complete sentences.

August groans again, curling himself tighter into a ball, deciding it wasn't cold enough to warrant abandoning the beanbag's warmth. Besides, after naptime came snack time, and he was very much looking forward to waking to a biscuit or two.

"Go on then. Get up." Mrs. Davies prods in her firm yet gentle way. The likes of which he ignores. "I said get up!" She strikes the desk with both palms, and the voice coming from her mouth is no more female than it is human.

The other students are sound asleep on their cots and do not see the eyes glaring at August. Neither does he at first. His back is to the aging educator, his arms hugging himself, and his eyes squeezed shut. But he sees them nonetheless in his mind, clear as daylight: two white spheres, devoid of pupils, set in a withering face.

He wants to shrink and continue shrinking until he becomes invisible. The classroom goes from a tolerable nippy to *mommy, I need a sweater* then to *lad, I hope you aren't as*

attached to your toes and fingers as they are to you.
"GET UP!"

AUGUST'S EYES fluttered open. Of all of the things that could have been real in his dream, the cold had been the realist. For a long moment, he stared through the gaping hole in the tin roof, watching snow sweep across the bright crescent moon. His fingers curled around the pendant lying on his chest. For a longer while still, there was a vacant look in his eyes bearing a striking resemblance to an Alzheimer's patient.

Where was he? Last he could remember was being somewhere else. A red place. *The* red place. Speaking words that did not belong to him, words he had no business speaking.

He remembered walking, balancing, on the rim of madness, then falling in. He remembered seeing *it*. The thing. The humanoid being seated at the head of a banquet table and the table dressed in fine linens.

At first glance, the table had offered a spread of delectable dishes. Roast pork belly, beef liver sautéed in onions and green peppers, thick slices of baked ham coated in a magnificent honey glaze, and beef wellingtons so rare you could hear them mooing. But like the table's hooded host, the food too had made August do a doubletake.

Upon closer inspection, he had come to realize that the food was not food. At least not the kind any human being should ingest. What appeared to be oven-roasted turkeys turned out to be human bodies separated from the torso just above the hips and the feet severed at the ankles. Frilly white booties had been placed at the ends to hide the unsightly boney knobs, but the calve muscles were a dead giveaway.

The brain wrestled with what the eyes saw, finding the roasting meat aroma tantalizing while his stomach had flip-flopped with the need to puke. August had torn his gaze away, but what they fell on next hadn't been better. Longer than the hours in the day and bone white, massive winding coils wriggled and slithered. They were the walls, the floor, the ceiling. A serpent's tail greater than any, originating from the host's Prussian blue robe.

There was one more thing he remembered. There had been a covered silver platter before the hooded being. He recalled its long arms stretching towards it. Longer than any man's arms. And how the albino limbs seemed to have manifested within the black pits of the robe's Prussian blue sleeves. The smooth scaly skin had shimmered like diamonds, a deceptive beauty.

When the lid came off, he had expected there to be another mutilated person. Instead, there had been a white rabbit. The critter sat there, twitching its nose and flicking its ears. Either too stupid or too ignorant to comprehend its impending demise. He had watched as one hand stroked the rabbit's back, and the other caressed its head, and in one jarring twist, it was dead.

August shuddered, recalling the audible crunch the rabbit's neck made. Then he shuddered again, replaying in his mind how the being lifted the limp rabbit by its cottontail and deposited it inside the dark void of its hood. The popping sound that followed had been like a snake unhinging its jaws.

"The Pale King." He uttered.

RUN RABBIT RUN

BEYOND THE moonlight's reach, August could hear something rustling in the surrounding shadows. He shut his eyes then opened them, fighting to free himself from the remnants of sleep's embrace. He felt rested and strange because of it. How long had it been since he'd experienced real sleep? The exact number of days eluded him. Days turned to weeks and weeks to months, and after a while, it had become impossible to keep track.

Everything blended together. Night was day, and day was night. The persistent insomnia had made him sickly, contributed to his aggressive weight loss, and kept his head in a fog. But now? Now that fog was gone. He could smell the cold air, the ripe stench of ammoniated piss, and faint traces of fecal matter.

Where had he wound up? Where were Reginald and Seko? *Seko*, he thought, clenching the pendant again. There wasn't an ounce of veil essence left in it. No sapphire glow either.

August willed himself to sit upright. The process took more effort than it had in the red place. In the dream, that hadn't been a dream at all. Oh, what he would give to be made whole in this world.

"Is someone there?" he asked, deer corn sifting through his fingers as he righted himself. Colorful beanbag chairs briefly came to mind. He concluded someone must have placed him on the pile of corn. But who? He did not believe the so-called veil-touched were responsible. Had they been, his hands and feet would surely be bound. Or worse, he'd be dead.

Had Seko done it? Reginald? There was no way the manservant would have willingly left his side. Was he dead?

Perhaps Reginald did die, and Seko left him here while she went to face the cultist freaks head-on.

No, that was impossible. Reginald could not die. August did not want him to be dead. And where exactly was *here* anyhow?

He looked around, spotted several wooden doors standing ajar. Each one was weathered by time and connected to an empty stall. He put two and two together. He hadn't been taken off the property after all. In fact, the opposite was true. Either Reginald or Seko had relocated him from the house to the stables where his grandfather once kept horses long before he was born.

Today the stables served as an impromptu storehouse. Tacked to the walls hung rusted chains with no discernible purpose, open barbaric beartraps hung on hooks looking like fossilized shark jaws, and miscellaneous landscaping equipment of a bygone era sat collecting dust.

Preoccupied with his thoughts, August was caught off guard by the rustling's return, louder this time and constant. "Look. I know someone's there. Show yourself already." *Someone* could very well be rats that made the stables their home for the winter, which explained why the piss odor was so robust.

No wheelchair, no crutches, but all human, he got to his feet, concentrating hard like a trapeze artist. In the dream that wasn't a dream, he discovered something about himself. He did not want to concede to death. At least not while lying on his back warm in bed, let alone a pile of deer corn, waiting for the inevitable to take him like a thief in the night.

He already beat the odds. Whatever greater power existed above had given him fifteen years. They weren't great years, nor were they terrible. They had been okay. Better than most people could hope for. So what if he didn't see the sixteenth? He would face whatever was to come in much the same way he had been forced to face the undead abomination on the beach.

Using one stall door after another for support, August crept his way towards the disturbance. Stubborn did not mean stupid. Nevertheless, as much as he would have liked to move undetected, the corn kernels crunching beneath his loafers gave him away. Abstract shadows stretched along the walls like daggers towards him but began to recede the closer he got, and the rustling became a distinct fluttering in his ears.

No, not here, he thought. There was no way an undead winged abomination made its way here. By the time he closed in on the sound's source, it had stopped. He did the same and listened. Standing in the moonlight, under the hole in the tin roof, he stared at the shadow three feet in front of him. His hand gripped the final stall door much tighter than he had the others.

For all August knew, he was confronting one of those tree things. Another birch golem with the ability to shapeshift like the one that passed itself off as his mother. "Go on then. Show yourself." His voice trembled.

There was nothing for a long while. Then as if realizing August wasn't going away, something did emerge from the shadows. He took a step back, head tilting up to see its face. He was confronted by the unexpected; no golem, no grotesque abomination, but a dark-skinned boy who stood a whole head taller than him, strong and healthy-looking.

He wondered if the boy was a Magpie like Seko. Perhaps the infamous veil-touched that had come to steal his life and blood? His face soured. "Who are you? Why are you trespassing on my property?"

"Nceda." The boy said in a tongue unfamiliar to August. His voice was a combination of human and something inhuman.

"What? I don't know what that means." He said, breath exiting his mouth in white puffs. However, to some degree, he felt he did know and shuddered. Goosebumps rose on his arms, hidden within the sleeves of his button-up. The boy took a step towards him, and he one back. "Stop. Don't come any closer. I'm warning you."

And if he did come closer, then what? Would August apply what he learned from his and Reginald's mock boxing and Jiu-Jitsu sessions? Could he? Because he knows in the real world, people don't hold back. They don't let you grab them or get a lick in to make you feel good about yourself. In the real world, people come at you with everything they got, and baby, you better be ready.

His words fell on deaf ears. The boy advanced. August braced himself, balled his hands into tight fists. He could see the boy was clutching something. By the time he made out what it was, it was too late, his fist already on a collision course with the boy's bare chest.

The light has a way of revealing gruesome truths. While not gruesome, the truth of the matter was the trespassing boy hadn't been clutching a weapon but his right arm. The shadows fell away from his umbra skin as the moon pointed its finger at the excessive amount of bright red blood running down the limp appendage. The look in his eyes, one August had mistaken for murderous intent, was terror.

His brain made the connection. The boy hadn't been lying in wait. He had been hiding, using the shadows as refuge, trusted them the way he once did. But hiding from what or whom?

August's fist faltered. The blow connected at half steam, overpowered by the strange boy's forward momentum. His wrist bent inward on itself, sending him staggering until his back struck the stall's exterior wall. There was no place for him to go but down. The boy slumped against him and the additional weight on his shoulders forced a knee to the cold clay floor. The pain was excruciating.

His hands clambered for something, anything, to bring him to his feet and found nothing. He twisted awkwardly, and with an exasperated sigh, freed his legs from under himself, planting his backside to the floor.

"You know, crushing me to death isn't going to help either of us," August said, using humor as a buffer to distract from his throbbing legs. It took considerable effort to prop the boy up. When he succeeded, they were more or less sitting side by side. He fumbled at his shirt buttons. "You sound a bit like a lady I know. Well, I don't really know her, to be fair. But I think I can trust her. Her name's Seko. Ring any bells?"

The boy did not answer. August supposed he hadn't expected him to. "You probably don't understand a word I'm saying." He shrugged, shucking the shirt off his shoulders as anxiousness substituted pain. "No matter. I can do enough talking for both of us. I rarely get to. Talk, I mean. I spend most my time cooped up like some bubble boy or listening to what others have to say. When someone does ask what I'm thinking, I don't know how to respond. I can no longer tell when someone's genuinely interested or just being nice. Why am I telling you all this? I guess I'm just tired, is all. Tired of being at the mercy of the world. Is that how you feel? Is that why you were hiding in the dark?"

August removed his shirt in less time than it had taken him to put it on. He had to be quick to stop the bleeding. In the process, he glanced the size tag in the shirt's collar. It read small. A weary smile creased his lips. *I guess there isn't much of me left*, he thought.

He folded the shirt. Then rolled it along his legs until it resembled a single piece of long cloth. "This is going to hurt," he warned, dabbing at the bloody bicep and finding the hole there. The wound gushed when pressed, but the boy did not react.

Never had August seen such dark skin on a person. If not for the moonlight, he would've overlooked the odd tattoos. Seeing them reminded him of the Rune Walker shaman he played in one of his RPG games. He carefully positioned the shirt behind the limb at the highest point above the wound, and icy fingers worked the two ends together, pulling as tight as his grip strength would allow. He got his reaction.

"Yima!" The boy hissed, grabbed him by the throat, and pressed his thumb hard to his windpipe.

"If I don't, you'll bleed to death." August wheezed. They locked gazes. He could see the boy's eyes were so brown they were almost black. He saw something else, too: fear and confusion. "I'm trying to help you. We can help each other."

"Nceda?" The boy questioned. He cocked his head in a way that was more befitting an animal than a person.

August tried to nod but couldn't. "Yes. I think?" There it was again. In less than fifteen minutes, he felt that invisible connection that tethered him to the boy. He knew he didn't mean to hurt him. He was reacting no differently than a dog would after having its tail accidentally trampled. How and why he comprehended this, he did not know.

The hand released him. He coughed and rubbed his bruised throat. "I'd appreciate you not doing that again." He said, reclaiming the ends of the shirt to start once more. "You'll have to help me. I only have two hands, and they aren't the best." Twice he wrapped it around the boy's arm then pulled tight, eliciting a pained grunt from his would-be patient. No more violence followed, and that was a good thing.

Hot blood soaked his fingers. They stuck together as he made one knot after another. He stopped all of a sudden, bloody fingers shaking and heart racing. He had forgotten something, a key component when it came to making a tourniquet. Something Reggie had shown him years ago.

What was it? What had he forgotten? Wrap the limb tight as high above the wound as possible, knot the material, then twist to stop the bleeding. It was simple, but it was also wrong. He had missed a critical step.

His eyes went to the boy's face, and what he saw set off alarm bells in his head. The boy looked pale (if such a word could be used to describe him), drained and eyes half-mast as if death itself was humming a sweet lullaby in his ear.

"Hey!" August shouted. The boy jerked awake. "Didn't I say that I needed your help? How can you help me if you're." *Dead* is the word he was about to say but refused. "If you're asleep, you're no good to me. I need you awake. Got it?" He also needed to remember what he had forgotten quick, fast, and in a hurry.

What he searched for clung to the tip of his tongue. Something that sounded like sash, lace, or lash, maybe. The harder he tried to remember, the more reluctant the word was to come. He had heard old people say if you leave whatever you're trying to remember alone that it will come to you when least expected. He needed it now. Right now.

Lash, he thought, rolling his tongue against the roof of his mouth. The word was right there, so close he could taste it. Lash. Lass. Windlass. The word was windlass. Or *twirly stick* as he liked to call it, knowing Reggie hated the term.

Right, without a windlass, a tourniquet wasn't a tourniquet. But where would he find one in a place like this?

August whipped his head over his shoulder. He saw nothing other than darkness. He considered the flashlight built into his mobile then realized he didn't have it. Even if he did, the thing wouldn't do him any good. It was fried courtesy of a weird electrical phenomenon.

He swept a hand behind him, searching the cold clay flooring and finding straw, corn kernels, and twigs too small to be of any use. He could get up, take a chance fumbling his way around, try to find something like a metal pin or a rod. Then again, how much time would that take? Just standing was a chore in and of itself, and without his crutches, one hell of a chore. The kind that gobbles precious minutes and makes people say never mind.

In about five minutes, the boy would bleed out. He felt useless. Fucking useless. He looked forward again at the boy who was easing ever closer towards eternal slumber. Now was the worst possible time to start feeling sorry for himself. His last name was Foxx and damn it all, he needed to act like it.

August's eyes lit up. "That! Give me that!" he pointed a boney finger. The answer hadn't been behind him but in front of him all along. Had it been a snake, it would have bitten him. He shook the boy. The response this time was no more than an unintelligible murmur. He was on his own.

Grunting, he leaned his torso across the boy's outstretched legs, fingernails scraping the ground like claws as he pulled himself towards what looked like a rat's nest in the making. One that, from the looks of it, had the misfortune of being visited by a prowling feline. He huffed, sucking cold air into his lungs. Adrenaline numbed him to the goose pimples breaking out along his exposed arms. He would later discover many cuts, scrapes, and purple bruises.

He heaved himself towards the disgusting bundle, something he would have never considered touching under normal circumstances. Tuffs of coarse hair—or maybe it was fur—combined with the pissy stench in his nostrils that muted all other smells were enough to make his skin crawl.

Fingers plunged in the soggy urine-caked filth, pulled it apart in clumps to claim his prize. There it was, what he had seen gleaming in the flickering moonlight. About the length of a number two pencil and black as obsidian stone, August clutched the broken antler. He had his windlass.

He wanted to admire the oddity. Instead, he scrambled back on his palms as best he could and apologized for the way his sharp knees and elbows dug into the other boy's legs. Panting, he stuck the antler between his lips and tried not to think about where it had been. Tingling hands repositioned the shirt above the gunshot wound, wrapped it tight, then tied the makeshift windlass in place, focusing in a way he never had before.

The toughest part for August was the twisting. The tighter he wound the antler, the more difficult it became for him to maintain a proper grip. His palms, beet red, felt nonexistent like sleeping limbs. This was the part where he needed help. Needed an extra hand to hold the windlass in place while he tied it off.

He pushed himself, twisted the antler a few more times for good measure. He was sweating, which was a death sentence in this cold.

"Hey! No sleeping, remember?" August jostled the boy and was relieved to find he was still breathing. "I need your help on this, you hear me? There's a handkerchief in my pocket." He had been meaning to return it to Reggie but hadn't gotten the chance. "I need to get it, and I need you to hold this while I do. I can't do both." He admitted with an ease and sternness that mirrored his father's.

August almost forgot about the language barrier between them, but with quick thinking, took the other's hand and positioned it on the makeshift windlass. He let go when he felt a squeeze of confirmation. "That's right. Just like that." He produced the handkerchief soiled with dry, dark blood splotches. His fingers, stiff and clumsy, fumbled to knot the handkerchief three times and nearly gave up on the fourth. On the seventh, he held his breath and pulled the knot tight.

The deed was done. August expelled a long sigh resting

his head on the stall's cool aged pine. From what he could tell, the strange boy was no longer bleeding. He could only hope he would hold on long enough to receive appropriate medical attention.

He looked down at his hands and tried to laugh but what came out was a hoarse, cracking sound. Red cuts flared, striping his grimy palms and fingers, and dirt caked under chipped fingernails. He felt alive. A bitter wind funneled through the hole above them, attacking his chest, bare shoulders, and arms. If he wanted to keep living, then staying put wasn't an option.

"How are you not freezing to death? I can barely feel my toes." August said, noticing the boy wore nothing more than a primitive-looking leather loincloth. "Either way, we can't stay here. I'm going to go find my friends. I'll come back for you, I swear it."

CHAPTER 19

THE AUG's TACTICAL FLASHLIGHT SWEPT over the front yard. Thick snow flurries fell across its wide beam. Reginald had convinced Seko to trade him the assault rifle for the Winchester, insisting that he needed to be point man on this. In his mind, he couldn't risk anything happening to her. The type of thought that could be interpreted as some misguided sense of chivalry yet was anything but.

In truth, they were leaving behind the sanctuary of the lodge to venture out into the unknown. For all Reginald knew, the night was not their alley, and they very well could be walking towards their deaths like lambs to the slaughter. A flashlight beam bouncing around in the dark was the best target any competent marksman could hope for.

Understanding the risks and being worse for wear

between himself and Seko, he did not mind playing the bait. If anything did happen to him, she would be granted a big enough window to respond, and he did not doubt that she would respond accordingly.

"How are you holding up?" Seko asked.

"Too soon to tell," Reginald said, scanning the yard. "Looks like the weatherman got it wrong." Earlier in the day, he cleared a path at the rear of the house when preparing for his and August's hunt. He had given the front the same treatment, clearing the steps leading to the circular drive. Looking at them now, it was like he hadn't done anything at all. No less than a foot of fresh powder coated them, and half as much occupied the neglected drive.

At the drive's center stood a three-tier granite fountain. In more agreeable weather, the fountain's basin would be surrounded by perfectly manicured grass encircled by boxwood hedges. However, having succumbed to the will of mother nature, the fountain resembled a snow-covered tower pointing to the sky.

Reginald tilted his head back to see the moon. It was barely a crescent yet glowed with an intensity that rivaled a floodlight. By midnight a new moon would be upon them, and all things would be shadow. He switched off the tactical flashlight. "The veil-touched, can they see in the dark?"

"For both our sakes, I hope not." Seko said.

Reginald looked at the rifle he held. The weapon felt at home in his hands but different somehow. Fresh in his mind, the ghoul's question lingered. Illusion or not, the answer he gave the undead boy had been the truth. For once, he did not feel like a soldier, did not feel like an angry man pointed at a target and told to shoot, no questions asked. The choice tonight was his and his alone to make.

To his left in the distance was a three-car garage. A Rolls Royce occupied one of the stalls. He knew this because he had parked the car there himself when they first arrived. In his mother's eyes, she would have taken the car as a sign of salvation, a ram in the bush meant to facilitate their escape out of this madness and back to a world that made sense. She would have been right.

"Do you see the garage over there?" Reginald said. "In it, there's a car. The keys are in my pocket. Once we have August, that's our ticket out of here. And if something were to happen to me, well, you know where the keys are."

Seko nodded. "You are sure we will find him at the stables? Interesting. I did not notice any signs of horses on the property."

"That's because there aren't any. Hasn't been for a long time. But it's the only building on the property with a metal roof, and that's what I heard when he fell. August and that *thing*."

Together Reginald and Seko descended the stairs. Snow and ice caked about his ankles, and moister seeped into his socks. Patent leather shoes, stylish as they were, offered little protection against a snowstorm, but he hadn't the time to change.

"That thing you are referring to, as I said before, is an impundulu. A lightning bird. A young one at that." Seko said.

"Ah, no wonder it struck me with lightning. It doesn't matter what it is, Ms. Seko. Like I said, if it bleeds, then it can die."

"Good point. Let me give you a better one. Do not forget that when you shot impundulu, it was in the back. Next time we may not be so lucky. All I am saying is keep both eyes open."

Reginald turned to Seko with his one good eye. His swollen lips stretched, forming a painful and ugly grin. "I shall do my best."

"You know what I mean."

He did know. Although, a small part of him wanted to continue believing that none of it was real. The idea that he'd finally had a psychotic break and was bouncing off the walls in some loony bin was a more comforting thought. About as comforting as knowing their supernatural attackers weren't impervious to bullets.

Still, he learned his lesson. The colossus taught him a thing or two about rushing in half-cocked like a maniac. Being an old emotional fool would only serve to send him to the grave. If not for Seko, he would already be a corpse. Alright then, fast and hard was not the way. Slow and steady wins the race.

Rifles at the ready, they trudged along. Snow crunched beneath their feet. In the process of leading them across the drive to the tree line, Reginald stopped and gestured with a hand for Seko to do the same.

"What is it?" She whispered.

Reginald gestured at his own eyes then pointed at the set of tracks in front of them. Fresh human tracks that the fast-falling snow had nearly erased. They had come from the tree line but, oddly enough, weren't pointed at the lodge. Instead, they broke off in the direction of the detached garage.

Dropping his stance, he raised the rifle and followed

alongside the footprints at a cautious pace, finger on the trigger as pain ping-ponged throughout his body. Seko followed his lead.

The tracks changed direction once more, crisscrossing as if the person they belonged to tried running and lost their footing in the process. Reginald's heartbeat quickened, the tracks leading them towards the towering fountain. He thought about the wide basin and how it could be used as cover to pick them off. But if that were true, then why not shoot them dead on the stairs? He knew the answer. To put it simply, shooting them in the back was the logical choice rather than engaging in an unnecessary and risky firefight.

In the distance, Reginald spotted movement and stopped. "Be ready." He said, swearing to himself he could feel a rifle's scope glaring at his forehead. He squinted with his right eye. About thirty feet ahead, he could make out what looked to be cloth blowing in the wind. "You see that? There's definitely someone there."

"Or something," Seko said. She disappeared in his blindside, and military intuition told him she was flanking the fountain. It was a smart yet risky move but a hell of a lot better than approaching together in a straight line like two dumb ducks.

Simultaneously they converged on the billowing white cloth as well as the person attached to it. Reginald went against his natural inclination to put two rounds in the threat at center mass. What stopped him was the fact the person did not appear to be moving. On top of that, he needed answers.

"Don't you fucking move." He commanded. He glanced at

Seko. Her face was hard, the Winchester gripped tight in her hands, and the barrel aimed at the person's chest. There was no missing at point-blank. Nevertheless, they both couldn't have their backs to the world. "Watch our six."

Reginald licked his cracked lips and stepped closer. Flipping on the flashlight, the grey digital patterns peppering the cloak jumped out at him. The figure wearing the winter camouflage was seated propped against the fountain's basin, head slumped forward, and both hands open-palmed at their sides. An Uzi submachine gun lay near the right, but a swift kick knocked it out of reach.

He steadied the AUG with one hand, and using the other, snatched off the hood. What he found beneath gave him pause. He brought the light closer, thinking the blow he'd taken to the head had his mind playing tricks on him. But no, it was there.

Wilting plant vegetation entwined stringy rust-colored hair matting a translucent scalp. On the face of it, one would assume the flowers had been braided by hand, the way a young maiden might in an attempt to capture the imagination of a suitor. It was the doubletake and the third that followed which told the truth. The truth being that the weird, freakish union of earth and flesh was skin deep.

The same hand closed around the ashen white mask, which depicted a beautiful woman's face encompassed by lush greenery, and lifted it. The face Reginald discovered was small, sunken-eyed, ears malformed and pointed, with green veins so pronounced he almost mistook them for tattoos or welts. He watched with astonishment as the entanglement of vines and leaves went from a lustrous green to shades of orange and brown like trees in autumn.

"She's dead," Reginald said. "But how?"

"Simple," Seko said. "I killed her."

"What?"

"The mark of the Green Woman is all over this one, and golems are complicated magic. To strike the heart of the child is to kill the mother."

Reginald gaped disbelievingly at the decomposing husk. *So, this is what a veil-touched looks like*, he thought. Something human and inhuman, beautiful and deadly. Nature's duality personified. "Such a tiny thing," he whispered.

"The veil takes its toll."

FREEZING FINGERS CLUNG to frozen tree bark to maintain his balance. Countless trees stood between the horse stable and the lodge. Five years had passed since August last visited the repurposed stables. Back then, there had been flat trails frequented by UTV. Today there were none.

Neglected and overgrown, no one tree was distinguishable from the last. Nightfall amplified the woods' disorienting power, and moonlight strained to breach the dense interwoven branches overhead. August felt a tinge of doubt, telling him he should have stayed put. Each step taken was a matter of life and death as snow devoured his legs up to the knees, constricting whenever he went to pull free.

Stubborn, he pressed on, lifting one leg and then the other, burning cold taxing his body's energy without remorse. His toes felt like small frozen meat logs, and now that the adrenaline had waned, he thought his fingers would break off.

RUN RABBIT RUN

August was tempted to raise his voice, call to Reginald and Seko but knew better. Not for a second had he forgotten that he was being hunted. Of all things pursued by cultist freaks, the kind that wasn't Kool-Aid drinking loonies, but the real deal. So real, every tree he grabbed made him think twice before grabbing it, convinced a birch golem would snatch him at any moment.

"I can do this," he chattered and kept moving. "I can do this. Do you hear me father? I'm not weak." His paranoia grew with the howling wind. He thought he heard something other than his shoes crunching snow and stopped. Had the strange boy decided to follow him? Dammit, all. He had told him to wait.

Expecting to confront the African teen, he whipped his head around. There was no one. Only the creaking and groaning gallery of trees watching him shiver and shake. He listened a while longer then started again.

A branch snapped. The sound was unmistakable as it bounced from tree to tree, making its origin impossible to pinpoint. August looked left, right, and behind him for the second time. He strained to see something, anything to indicate whether or not he was alone. He thought about wolves. This far north, the idea of wolves in the area wasn't outside the realm of possibility. To think he survived mutated undead birds and demonic golem creatures only to be done in by a pack of overgrown dogs.

The wind whipped hard against his face. The snow it carried stung like tiny ice needles. He wrapped his arms around himself despite needing his hands free to navigate between the trees. A creaking sound caught his attention, but this time he did not look around. He did something most people never do. He looked up.

In the treetops where the moon was brightest, August saw movement. Bare branches swayed hypnotically, and he almost swayed with them. A greyish-silver glint caught his eyes. He thought it an owl or some other bird until he saw it again. His heart leaped into his throat. What he was looking at was clothing with some kind of reflective piping.

August played it cool, turned slowly, pretended not to see what his eyes saw. But he couldn't leave it at that. The hairs on the back of his neck begged him to turn around. And so he did, whipping his head so hard he thought he might break his neck in the process. The figure outlined by glinting, greyish silver scurried further up into the trees. Its movement non-human.

He yelped in utter terror as he watched the thing leap effortlessly from one branch to another. The tree he pressed to trembled, showering him in twigs, snow, and ice, marring his shoulders with fresh cuts and bruises. Fear paralyzed him until a deafening crack thawed his legs. He uprooted one foot at the cost of a shoe, half running, half hobbling to escape what was to come.

His mouth was dry, hands clammy, and his heart pounding so hard in his chest he could feel his pulse throbbing in his ears. August didn't get far at all. He stumbled over his legs like a good-for-nothing cripple and faceplanted nose-first in the snow. The ground quaked under the mighty crashing branch, spraying snow, ice, and splintered wood in every direction. He shielded his head with his hands.

Something else landed nearby. The world grew still, changed, choked by an unpleasant presence that made August's skin crawl. He felt compelled to look. Had to see, had to know. He lifted his head and opened his brown eyes.

"Hello, little rabbit." The voice that spoke was venom, a thick molasses that filled the nooks and crannies of his mind. His vision focused. Mere inches from his face, there was another, whiter than white, void of human features, sporting two black pits for eyes. He shrieked, scampering back awkwardly. But there was no place to run, let alone hide. "For an invalid, you have been a thorn in my side. She keeps protecting you. But that's because she doesn't know any better. But she will soon."

August stared wide-eyed at the blank face for a long while before understanding that it wasn't a face but a mask. An expressionless visage that was both mysterious and chilling. "Who are you?" he said, finding the courage to speak.

"You should be asking yourself that question. Who *are* you?" The figure rose to an impressive height. White hooded cloak billowed on the wind. Whomever this person was dressed in full military garb on par with Royal Marine Spec Ops. He did not see a gun amongst the many pouches or a holster, for the matter. He did see a knife and swallowed hard.

Gloved fingers wrapped around the knife's handle. The very same handle Seko had shown to August before. He did not need to see it up close to know the carving was there: the buck and the maiden. Unsheathed, the blade shined like a long angry fang.

August quivered. "You're a crazy person."

"Oh, you know better than that little traveler." The figure approached, brandishing the knife.

August felt ill. He sat upright, pressed his back to the tree. *Don't piss yourself*, he thought. *Don't give this fuck the satisfaction.*

"You've been places. You've seen things." The trespasser was right. He had been to places and seen things. Awful things that should not be allowed to exist. Things that came close to killing him and ruining his life. "You know what your blood means to us. You know that you are both door and key."

Strong fingers fisted August's hair, wrenched it hard, used it to drag him to his feet. Anger and pain flashed in those brown eyes of his. If he had heat vision, whatever face was behind the mask would have been burned to a crisp.

"I'm done being afraid of you," August said, a half-truth. "You're nothing but a pathetic lackey. Do you really think the Pale King gives a toss about you? He's using you, and you're too daft to know it. And you smell sick like you're dying or something. Just another body for his army, another undead freak."

The trespasser seemed to weigh his words before pressing the blade to his exposed throat, breaking the skin. "Little rabbit, I don't need you to be afraid. I just need you to die so that we may live."

He was at a loss for words. Then it hit him that there was nothing he could say to prolong the inevitable. The half fear he had settled for regressed into despair. He lowered his gaze, blinked. Around the trespasser's neck hung a beaded necklace, pulsing subtly with symbols identical to the strange boy's tattoos.

"It won't be long now." The trespasser said. "Soon my sisters will return and you will spill the blood of red and white. We will be a family again."

The words rang with familiarity. August saw images of the beach, the raging bonfire, and the heinous acts performed on the bound man through whose eyes he had spectated. The trespasser withdrew the blade from his throat and made a motion to grab him, perhaps take him, someplace where they would wait for the so-called sisters to come molest and kill him in their perverse ritual.

A gunshot boomed. August nearly jumped out of his skin. The trespasser fell against him and he shoved them away with all the strength he could muster.

"August!" A voice that sounded like gravel pierced the night. He could see light in the distance. It bobbed up and down, growing in size and power as it drew nearer. "August!" The voice shouted once more, closer now.

"Here. I'm here!" August tried shouting himself, his words a brittle rasp. "Over here. I'm here."

Reginald exploded from the darkness, his light blinding. "August. Are you alright?"

August tried to answer. His legs gave. He slid down the base of the tree rubbing at his throat with a trembling hand. "I think so." He choked, fighting back tears.

"Butler. Give me light." Seko demanded. Her attention was on the ground. Reginald hesitated, straightened, then did as instructed.

There the trespasser lay face down, the knife jutting from the snow beside them. Seko stepped forth and drove her foot into their side. A second well-placed kicked turned the trespasser over, and in the twinkle of an eye, something metallic flickered in the moonlight. Reginald snarled, grabbed his throat with both hands, and staggered back. The submachine gun hit the snow and mounted flashlight streaked the woods with long, lurid shadows.

"Reggie!" August cried.

Seko had the trespasser dead to rights and pulled the Winchester's trigger. *Click!* A misfire. The trespasser was on their feet, grabbed the rifle, and a tussle ensued. It ended as quickly as it began. In a spray of blood and spittle, the butt of the rifle cracked Seko across the jaw, sending her whirling.

The trespasser spun the rifle in spectacular fashion. Once repositioned in their hands, Seko was the one on the receiving end. *Click!* Another misfire. August recalled the gun doing the same thing to him when he and Reginald had been hunting. The rifle was far from broken. The problem was that neither Seko nor the trespasser had squeezed the lever hard enough to release the firing mechanism.

Reginald charged in like a bull, throwing blinding haymakers. The trespasser slipped each blow, their movement fluid yet abnormal like a person who had precognitive abilities. The manservant threw a left, right, back-to-back straight jabs too quick for August to track in the low light. The trespasser dodged them all, bobbing and weaving the man's raging fists.

The gap between them increased, and all of a sudden, the trespasser spun, flipped the rifle in hand, and used it like a club bashing the manservant across the back. Reginald howled. He stumbled forward, collapsed to a knee, expelling ragged breaths. He tried to get back up but failed. The trespasser raised the rifle and aimed.

RUN RABBIT RUN

When the trespasser pulled the trigger, the sound the Winchester made split the sky wide open. The bullet impacted the tree beside August's head, exploding wood and ice, and fresh blood warmed his face. His flinch, a delayed reaction.

Seko had intervened, sparing one life and nearly costing August his. She had deflected the rifle, grabbed it, but dropped it in the scuffle. Neither she nor the trespasser chased after the long gun. She unleashed a flurry of punches. Each one blocked, dodged, and countered in grand style.

A well-timed back fist put a stop to Seko's forward momentum. She was stunned but recovered quickly, throwing a spinning heel kick that sent the trespasser's mask flying. The two engaged again, but Seko was slowing down, limping. She threw another punch. The trespasser caught it and twisted her wrist with a resounding crunch. She hollered.

The trespasser slapped Seko across the face then backhanded her for good measure. She sagged to the ground, her wrist remaining captive as the moon blinked from the sky. The only light that remained came from the partially buried flashlight.

August knew he had to do something. But what? He looked around frantically. About ten feet from where he was, he saw the answer.

He flopped onto his belly and began to crawl towards the muffled light. Ten feet may as well have been ten miles. August couldn't feel his fingers or toes at all. What he could feel was the sharp pain between his shoulders and the deep ache in his hips and legs.

Hurry, he told himself. He had to hurry or Seko and Reggie were going to die. If they died, that meant it was all over, meant this entire realm was doomed like the red place. Unfeeling hands clawed the winter white, drug himself forward, pushing his upper body strength to its limitations. Labored breaths misted the air and building mucus rattled his chest.

Reaching the light source August began digging with single-minded determination and did not stop until he struck paydirt. He excavated the assault rifle, gripped it tight, and rolled over, sneering. "Stop it!" He tried shouting. The words came out a hoarse snarl.

In his hands, the rifle did not tremble, did not shake, did not quake. The tactical flashlight, bright as dawning daylight, revealed the trespasser to him as well as Seko on her knees about to be executed. He saw Reginald lying face down, unmoving. "I said stop it, or I *will* fucking kill you."

August had the trespasser's attention. The knife held at Seko's throat had drawn blood. A much smaller blade in comparison to the one used on him. The same kind that he surmised was used to attack Reggie.

The trespasser turned to look at him. What the light revealed was gruesome. The trespasser was a woman and not a pretty one either. Where her right eye should have been, there was thick scar tissue instead. Her left eye a cloudy jade sphere. The skin on the left side of her face appeared melted, burnt. He remembered her, the squawking gulls, and blistering bonfire.

"Well, now. Look at that sneer. The monster inside the boy shows itself." The trespasser said, her venomous voice went hand in hand with her hideous mug.

"You're one to talk." August said.

"And you should be one to listen. Do you even feel anything for them? I mean truly feel. Or are you acting on impulse? Doing what you think you're supposed to do because it's morally right?"

"I'm warning you."

"Do it, August. Kill her." Seko moaned.

The trespasser tightened her grip. "I have seen dynasties fall. Men and women shackled and chained. I was there when the shamans burned. I whispered in the ears of kings. Do you think you can kill me? My sisters? To take what is ours with impunity? We waited so long for this night. We grew desperate as our numbers dwindled. Made a pact with Him to prolong our lives in exchange for you. In exchange for a chance to claim our recompense."

"You failed," August said. He squeezed the trigger, tried to squeeze the trigger. The AUG's trigger pull weight was heavier than the Winchester's had been. It didn't budge. His face screwed up as his brain commanded a finger he couldn't feel to pull the damned trigger.

The trespasser chuckled darkly. "There are cultures where you would have been thrown off a cliff at birth." August knew her words aimed to hurt him, but he was too tired and too angry to be wounded. It was frustration and hopelessness that rimmed his eyes with hot tears.

A gale-force wind descended on them so abruptly there was no time for August to react. It sounded like a freight train barreling through the trees. The might of it compelled August to bow while the trespasser struggled but remained rooted on her feet. Just as quickly as it had come, the freakish winds dissipated.

"About time you arrived." The trespasser said. "Your passive-aggressive acts of defiance are starting to wear my patience. Now bring me the boy." Her cloudy green eye turned to August. "As for you. Don't go putting up a fuss, or I'll slit your little bird's throat."

August was convinced Seko was doomed whether he cooperated or not. Cautiously he raised his head. Eyes hotter than the sun stared down at him.

"Oh no." Seko grimaced. "Get away from him, creature. August, you must get away."

August did not attempt to flee. He sat up a little straighter, head tilted back as he stared up into the familiar yet changed face. It was him. The strange boy. The African teen. "You remember me, don't you?"

"I'm not going to repeat myself." The trespasser said, puncturing Seko's neck. Blood began to flow.

Electricity sizzled, crackled, and popped along the boy's body. To August, he looked like a living Tesla coil. In unison, he and the boy fixed their gazes on the trespasser. He dropped the gun and half raised his hands in the universally understood gesture of surrender.

Despite his tears, August grinned. Grinned because around his wrist dangled the necklace the trespasser had been wearing. He snatched it when she had gotten shot and fallen against him. Her expression was dumbstruck.

Before the trespasser could utter another word, the boy outstretched an arm towards her. Electricity traveled along the appendage in rings. He extended his index finger, pointed it. A single bolt of lightning lit up the night as if a flashbang grenade had gone off.

RUN RABBIT RUN

August's whole world went white then black.

AUGUST AWOKE WITH a start. His ears were ringing and the world a black shroud over his eyes. He thought he had gone blind, but the light he saw flickering in his peripheral told him otherwise.

"Reggie? Seko?" August shouted, unable to hear the sound of his own voice. In vain, he tried again, the ringing in his ears a constant drone that assaulted his equilibrium. He rolled to his side in the light's direction, his head lulling, and the world went spinning out of control.

He shut his eyes and kept them shut until the moment passed. When he opened them, he stared straight ahead. The flashlight flickered on and off like an SOS broadcast. His eyes followed its path to where a person lay in the snow.

At first, he thought they were dead. Then he saw the shallow rise and fall of their chest. August pressed himself flat to the ground, his elbow bumping something, and his hand reached for it without thinking. He began to crawl too without thinking, clawing the earth with one hand and fisting it with the other, not wanting to drop what he found.

The closer he got, the clearer the reflective camouflage pattern became. What else became clearer was the god-awful stench of burnt flesh. Nevertheless, the urge to vomit did not strike him. He came upon the trespasser. Her face burnt beyond recognition and her clothing fused to her body.

August climbed on top of her, straddled her, staring down at that one cloudy eye. It didn't stare back. If anything, it looked through him, but he did not care. He raised the knife, watched what was left of the trespasser's lips move, and for a long while, couldn't hear a word. The ringing in his ears persisted, then all of a sudden, it stopped. He could hear everything.

"Matilda. Ula. Forgive me. I can't see your faces. I can't smell the sea." The trespasser mumbled.

August buried the knife in her throat. Her lips continued to move, so he dislodged it and repeated the act. The blade scraped bone, but even then, he couldn't stop. Anger and hatred flashed in his eyes as he cut, slashed, and stabbed. Hot blood covered his hands and speckled his face. He didn't know he was screaming, wailing at the top of his lungs like a wild beast. What he did know is that he needed the trespasser to be dead. Permanently. Forever and always.

Hands grabbed August from behind and hoisted him in the air. He flailed. "Hey. I got you. You are all right. Do you hear me? You are all right. Be still now. Seko has you."

All at once, August felt utterly exhausted and began to sob. Together they sank to the ground.

"We need to go. We have to get back to the house." Seko said, stroking his hair.

"No. Not without Reggie." August said.

"I am sorry. I am afraid he did not make it."

"Then we need to leave. Reggie wouldn't want us to stay here. He would say it's not safe."

"The house is the safest—"

"No. I want to leave right now. Do you understand me? I want to leave this place."

"How? There is nowhere to go. We go back to the house and wait for sunrise."

"There's a car. Reggie always keeps the keys on him no matter what."

Seko said nothing. She sat for a second longer, then got up and walked to where the manservant lay. August watched her. He wiped tears from his eyes, smearing blood across his face in the process.

The woman stooped, checked one pocket after another. Her startled cry disrupted the heavy silence that had settled the woods. August tensed. He squinted and saw the large hand wrapped around Seko's wrist. A familiar baritone voice spoke.

"Not. Dead. Yet."

CHAPTER 20

REGINALD USED THE MANUAL KEY to unlock the Rolls. When he had tried the SUV's electronic key fob, he got nothing more than a weak chirp, and the Spirit of Ecstasy did not rise.

"I'll take him. Here. Start the car." Reginald said, panting. He exchanged with Seko the key for August, who she had carried piggyback to the garage. He hadn't the strength to do it himself. His head was spinning, pounding, and he concentrated hard to wield the world to be still.

"Wait. There was a boy. Did you see him?" August asked, teeth chattering.

Reginald suppressed the urge to nod. He carefully placed his ward in the rear passenger seat. "I did. That thing was no boy. It tried to kill us. We need to go before it or more of those masked wearing freaks decide to show up."

"We can't just leave him. If it weren't for him, we'd all be dead."

Reginald gave him a questioning look. "You must've hit your head. I'm telling you that thing tried to kill us. I've got the burn marks to prove it." He reached across August, fumbling for the safety belt.

August resisted, fighting off his hands. "I didn't hit my head. I know what I saw. He was in about as much trouble as we were. He helped us."

"I can't take that risk." Reginald snapped. "Every minute we stay here is a minute where our lives are in danger."

"I'm not asking." August said. His words came out slurred.

"He is gone." Seko broke in. "The boy, impundulu, he is gone. Whatever was tethering him to the witch, he took it and left. I did not comprehend at first, but I saw. Your friend will live to see another day."

"Are you sure?" August asked.

Seko nodded.

Reginald felt August's grip on his forearm relax. "Then it's settled. Start the car, Seko. We're leaving."

"I am sorry. I cannot do that." Seko said.

"What are you talking about?" Reginald said as he fastened August's seatbelt.

"The safest place for the boy to be is here. Going out into the world right now is not safe for any of us."

"What would you have us do, sit around like cavemen in the dark sharpening our spears waiting for whatever's to come? There are no phones. No power here. We drive to Redbreast and sort things out there." Reginald was about to stand but froze when he heard the all too familiar sound of the AUG's slide racking.

"Have you gone mental?" August slurred, teeth chattering.

"Sit back." Reginald pressed his palm into the boy's chest, forcing him to comply. His wide back took up most of the SUV's doorway as he remained down on one knee. "Ms. Seko, you're making a mistake. We all want the same thing here. I get it. We're all wound a bit tight and want tonight to be over." He looked at August and August back at him. "We've got to trust one another."

"Take the boy out the car. We are going back inside." Seko said.

"Why are you doing this? You know we can't stay here." August said, shaking like a leaf. Reginald would have liked nothing more than to crank the car and get the heat going.

"Don't you worry, Master August. Everything's going to be fine," Reginald said. He reached for the safety belt's release then past it. His hand unsteady as callused fingers groped for the passenger armrest, which was barely visible in the car's underpowered cabin light.

"My mission is to protect the boy. To keep him here and keep him safe." Seko said.

Reginald guardedly opened the armrest. "Ms. Seko, I learned a long time ago that there's a distinct difference between a mission and commonsense." His vision went in and out of focus. A hand grabbed to steady himself, but he collapsed, slumping against the door and clutching his right side.

"We need to get him to hospital!" August panicked.

RUN RABBIT RUN

Reginald listened. He could hear the woman's fast-approaching footfalls. The sound the rifle made as she raised it. The deafening *BANG! BANG! BANG!* Heat scorched his right side. He did not have to look to know what had transpired. He could feel it. The heat. The blood. The pain.

"Don't be afraid," Reginald puffed. "What do you say we head on down the road?" The expression on August's face was a cocktail of shock, horror, and bewilderment. Reginald used the side sill to anchor himself before standing. In his right hand, he clutched the 9mm Browning.

"Is she dead?" August hesitated to ask.

"Sit back," Reginald said, shutting the door. He did not want the boy to see. *Are you death?* The question resurfaced as he turned on his heels to face his handiwork. *What a waste*, he thought as his eyes passed over what remained. He noted the blood pooling in Seko's abdomen, the hole in her neck, and she now had one eye instead of two. The left had been blown clean out of its socket. The right was without expression. She hadn't seen it coming.

Reginald picked up the AUG and got in the car. He placed the rifle on the passenger seat and the Browning on the armrest long enough to adjust the rearview mirror. August was watching him and their eyes met. "Won't be long now. I promise." He said.

August did not respond. He could see in the boy's puffy eyes something he had experienced for himself more than once in his life. First, under his parents' roof, again in the Brixton riots, and thirdly when he served overseas. What he saw was unmistakable and undeniable shellshock.

Reginald wanted to comfort him. He couldn't. The best thing he could do right now was drive. Drive far away from this place, effectively putting the whole ugly business behind them.

He touched his side, fingered where the bullet had grazed him when he fired the pistol. He winced. It had been a reckless thing to do. But in the heat of the moment, no better alternative came to mind.

Reginald put his foot on the brake and pressed the ignition button. The cabin lights brightened, a rapid clicking commenced, then the lights dimmed again. He punched the steering wheel before squeezing it with both hands. "This one thing. I just need this one thing." He muttered through gritted teeth. "I know you been looking out for me, mum. Praying for me. I know I don't deserve it, but I'm not asking for me. Please. Just this one thing."

He pressed the ignition button. The cabin lights brightened, the pretentious chimes played their little melody, and the V12 engine roared to life.

In less than ten seconds, the SUV was plowing through the snow like a battering ram. Reginald's foot feathered the accelerator letting the weight of the Rolls do the heavy lifting. They were practically sailing down the drive's two-mile stretch. The trees passing them on either side seemed to bid them farewell.

He stole multiple glances in the rearview. August looked like death warmed over. The boy had removed his seatbelt and was curled in the fetal position. All the signs were there; shivering, exhaustion, slurred speech. Clear indicators of hypothermia. "Master August," Reginald called. "Don't you go drifting off on me. You're a tough lad. You stay with me, you hear? Stay with me."

Subconsciously he further compressed the accelerator. The V12 responded with a throaty growl. He activated the climate control and cranked up the heat. But the fan settings he kept relatively low as not to blast his ward with more freezing cold air.

Reginald absently scanned the analog clock integrated in the dash. It read one minute 'til midnight. "Happy early birthday. You see that? In one minute, you'll be sixteen. In one minute, you'll beat the odds. What do the doctors know? Nothing, that's what. You've come too far, Master August. You've come too far to give up now. So don't you close your eyes. Don't you go to sleep just yet."

One hand gripped the wheel tighter. Reginald used his other hand to undo his shirt, thumbing loose one button after the other, all the while casting concerned glimpses in the rearview. He wondered if it would be enough. It had to be. It just had to be enough until they were far from the lodge and he could safely pull to the side of the road. Seeing August lying there weak and becoming weaker by the second made him want to press the accelerator not to the floor but through it.

He got a hold of himself. His fingers moved posthaste, popping buttons undone. He hit a snag, improvised by ripping his shirt open, sending buttons flying and ricocheting every which way. The seatbelt chime's rebuke was a constant, but he ignored it as he shrugged the shirt off his broad shoulders. He got an arm free, switched steering hands, and looked in the rearview mirror for the umpteenth time. What Reginald saw chilled his bones to the marrow.

August had shut his eyes. At a glance, Reginald couldn't tell if he was breathing. He whipped his head around, reached into the backseat grabbing the boy's knee, and shook him. "August," he said, dropping the formalities. "August, you got to stay awake. August? Do you hear me?"

The boy did not stir and touching him was like touching a block of ice. Reginald felt a heavy weight form in the pit of his stomach. Sweat beaded his forehead and his heart hammered. *This cannot be*, he thought, staring at his ward's slack face. He looked unnatural, doll-like.

"You're not dead. You hear me? You're not dead. Wake up dammit!" He shook August some more. Shook him hard before forcing himself to face forward. His eyes threatened tears. He pressed his lips together into a fine tight line seeing the road ahead but not really. When he did see it, his whole body tensed, and his heart skipped several beats.

In the center of the drive stood the tallest buck Reginald ever laid eyes on. Taller than eight feet. Its pelt, black as oil, absorbed the Xenon headlight beams like a blackhole. Its head donned huge antlers that twinkled like polished steel. The points of which were impossible to count at a glance, but there were many.

The buck was staring right at him. Its bright green eyes full of intelligence. Green eyes. A deer with green eyes and a pelt black as tar.

Reginald processed all of this in less than two seconds before jerking the wheel left to avoid collision. The SUV banked hard. The tires lost traction on a patch of black ice, catapulting them into a three-hundred and sixty-degree spin. He removed his foot from the gas, tried to counter steer, but was too far gone.

The SUV's right side slammed into a tree in an explosion of glass. Reginald's head bounced off the driver's side window cracking it, his left arm made a terrible crunching sound, and his face impacted the steering wheel so hard the horn bleated. Not a single front cabin airbag deployed.

He sat there, mental faculties intact, listening to the wind howl. He tried to breathe but wheezed. The blood accumulating in his mouth told him what he needed to know. He had punctured a lung and seemed he would choke to death on his own blood. All the same, he needed to move, needed to open the car door, needed to check on August. What he soon realized was more disheartening than a punctured lung.

In a matter of seconds, Reginald had become a prisoner in his own body. He thought the obligatory thoughts, tried to wield himself to wiggle the proverbial big toe as the Bride had done in Tarantino's Kill Bill. But the body was no more willing than it was able.

He felt warm air on his face, out of the blue yet gentle. The air became a breeze that carried him away to the summer of 1982. He could hear his dad's voice. The man spoke to him and his brother as they walked the forest. They stalked a buck Reginald would later shoot that afternoon.

The world had been big then the way it sprung up all around him in shades of green, brown, and grey. The pine was almost overpowering after the light rainfall. He stared up into his dad's face, up because he was not yet a man of six feet two inches tall, but a boy aged thirteen. A boy who will file the day's events away like a polaroid in a photo album and will revisit the memory thirty-six years later when it's his turn to show compassion.

Reginald listened to his dad teach them the facts of life using deer stalking as an analogy. Listened and watched the man show and tell the proper way to track a buck. Despite the rain, he saw no storm clouds in his dad's eyes. Of this, Reginald was glad. He appreciated it the way a fish appreciates water.

The forest slowly dissolved and he was back behind the wheel of the mangled SUV. His head lay on the steering wheel, staring blankly out the shattered driver's side window. Back at him stared a single cue ball-sized glowing green eye. The beast behind the eye snorted. It spoke to him. Not orally, but it spoke.

Reginald heard two voices in his head speaking in unison. The voices sounded like thoughts to him, but he knew they were something more. Something greater than himself. Greater than man.

You have fulfilled your purpose. Rest well.

CHAPTER 21

FLOATING. IT FELT LIKE FLOATING. He had wondered what death would be like. In cinema, death is too often romanticized. Terms such as *a good death*, *a warrior's death*, and *a clean death* are a constant on script pages.

Warmly lit scenes illustrate family members gathered around a loved one's hospital bed, and everyone gets to say their goodbyes. A hero's closest confidant is mortally wounded, and with his or her final breaths, they speak the words that stoke the fires of vengeance the hero needs to carry on. No one ever mentions the pissy death, the shit-stained death, or the scared shitless death. Cinema experiences like that weren't blockbuster material.

August had come to grips that people who did not have to think about their mortalities seldom did. Life had its way of reminding such people just how fragile it is through the universally recognized and jelly-leg-inducing *close call*. Having agonized over death for years, he had never needed any such reminder. The seed had been unintentionally planted by their family physician Dr. Paul Adjei.

The good doctor had stood outside his bedroom door in conversation with his parents. The man had spoken quietly (or so he had tried) with Robert and Veronica hanging on his every word. August had been hanging on too, straining his ears not to miss a single syllable.

"I'm sorry. I truly am. But nor my colleagues or I have ever encountered anything like this before. Whatever August has, checks all the boxes for polio, but it isn't that. His aggressive insomnia isn't helping either. He needs rest and plenty of it. I know the medication he was on before didn't agree with him. I will prescribe him something less abrasive to help him sleep. If not, there's just no telling. He could be here today and gone tonight."

Here today, gone tonight. Here today, gone tonight. Here today, gone tonight. The words stuck with August, haunted him, visited him in the late-night hours.

He needn't worry about all that now. Whatever renewed vigor he had acquired at the stables was knocked out of him in the crash. Hypothermia latched its hooks into him and he had shut his eyes to sleep the deep slumber.

No family members surrounded him. No opportunity to exchange goodbyes. No friend who would exact revenge in his name. There was only the black void. A cold emptiness where the voices no longer gnashed at him.

RUN RABBIT RUN

August floated weightlessly through its vast expanse. Not quite flying, but drifting peaceably the way a log would down a lazy river. There were the occasional dips and bobs. Trumpets trumpeted a benign melody that beckoned him to come forth and come home.

He wanted that more than anything. To come home, to be home, to be somewhere he belonged and whole. Faint voices harmonized. The frequency at which they vibrated seemed to birth tiny light orbs, fuzzy and out of focus. Were they souls? If so, was he destined to be like them, a ball of energy bouncing around in oblivion?

The lights intensified, dwindled, intensified, dwindled. August felt afraid. A sensible fear that told him he was approaching the point of no return. The end of a thing and the start of something else. The light at the end of the tunnel.

The lonely cold became a receding tide replaced by a creeping warmth. The feeling pacified August's woes. It coursed through him like a fever. Fingers and toes tingled with an awakening that said *we're here*. For the longest, he hadn't felt anything other than raw emotions.

He continued to float, ascending. A dull pain reanimated his limbs, telling him that he was alive. He could hear an electric current buzzing. He felt light on his eyelids, soft then intense. He tried opening them. An arduous undertaking, but he succeeded.

What August saw was a series of hazy octagonal shapes. When they came into focus, he found himself gazing upon the face of the lodge. The log house looked alien as it towered above him in all its grandeur. Power had been restored and every window lit. The structure looked like a living, breathing thing.

He became aware of something else. He wasn't standing on his own two feet. What he had perceived as floating was someone carrying him in their arms. He wanted to look over his shoulder. Wanted to see who the person was. Fatigue denied him, and again the abnormal warmth pacified his woes.

August was carried through the tall double doors. An eerie stillness hung in the air. Thoughts of Reginald and Seko were fleeting and without grief. He felt drunk, not at all himself, and drained. It was as if his mind were enveloped by a thick fog.

They covered the distance from the front entrance to the elevator located at the center of the house. The metallic door slid open without pressing the call button. August was carried inside. Only then was he placed on his feet. He wobbled. A hand placed on his shoulder steadied him.

He did not think to ask questions, protest, or fight. Docile as a lamb, he studied his reflection in the elevator's surrounding reflective metal panels. There was a bluish tint to them that was vaguely aquatic. Congealing blood coated his face, neck, and hands. Some of it was his, but most of it belonged to the stranger. His clothes hung on him, filthy, soaked through by water that had been snow and ice.

A hand clad in a white cloth glove pressed the elevator's bright red stop button then twisted it like the dial on a combination lock. The stop button popped open, revealing the keyhole hidden behind it. When a key was inserted into the hole and turned, the elevator did not ascend as it should have but descended.

RUN RABBIT RUN

The figure knelt in front of August as the elevator began its descent. It was a man dressed in a two-piece black suit, white button-up shirt, and black necktie. The man's face was hidden behind a crude wooden stag mask.

The man did not speak. What he did do was remove August's ruined undershirt by pulling the garment off overhead. His trousers were unbuttoned next, unzipped, and pushed down to his ankles. The man moved with a clinical detachment that suggested he had done this before. When finished, August was left standing naked as a robin, and the abnormal warmth pacified his woes.

CHAPTER 22

THE ELEVATOR CAR CAME TO a smooth stop. The doors yawned open. Saying not a word, the masked man stepped out and gestured for August to do the same. He did, trading the elevator's artificial light for the subterranean torch-lit stone passage.

An earthy smell invaded August's nostrils. There was a pure quality to it. The passage was unmarred by man's smokestacks and combustion engines and gave off the impression of being very old, akin to the catacombs in Paris.

How deep underground was he? This is the question August would have asked himself if not for the dreamlike haze permeating around him. He was keenly aware of his environment but unable to react to it: zombified.

He shuffled obediently in his mute chaperone's footsteps.

Another man awaited them who dressed the same as the first. But unlike the first man, he wore an entire deer's head, and black unblinking eyes stared at August where human eyes should have been. The man carried something in his hands and came forward. The undulating torchlights gave the object the appearance of a crown forged from shadow with raised, exaggerated points.

Goose pimples broke along August's naked flesh. He was brought eye-to-eye with what the man held, knew what it was because it was he who had taken the beast's life. He gawked at the buck's decapitated head. While its eighteen-point antlers remained intact, the bottom jaw had been removed and the head hollowed out, resembling a bastardized rendition of something Peter Pan's Lost Boys would wear.

The man stepped behind him, and he felt the weight of the buck's antlers and half-head come down on his. The first man knelt before him once more. Draped over an arm was a thin fabric, neatly folded and covered in short reddish-brown hair. Just as he had been undressed, the same impersonal touch was used to secure the fabric around his waist. A long strip hung down, covering his loins and backside.

From the rear, a second piece of hide was laid across August's shoulders, pinned in place by an antler cast in pure gold that was closer to branching tree than bone. Bits of fat and flesh clung to the hide, sweated in the passage's humidity.

To his left, he could hear muffled voices vocalizing. The very same voices he had heard when outside the lodge. A silent chaperone flanked him on either side. Each man gestured an arm in the direction from which the voices came.

August sensed what they expected of him. He turned his head towards the specified path. As he did, a whistling wind caressed his face with a heat that rivaled sunlight in summer. He could hear hooves clopping at his back, but they seemed unimportant. His brown eyes homed in on what was.

The torches lining the walls were his visual guide. Showed him the green vines inhabiting the passage and how they pulsed subtly. Behind August, the vines went on for miles. In front of him, they went no further than fifty feet.

Entire sections of stone flooring were inundated with climbers. But it wasn't the trailing plants that commanded his attention. Where they ended, a solitaire Prussian blue door towered, haloed by a high stone archway.

The door must have been thirty feet tall, give or take. A blue obelisk that stood out amongst corroding stone and framed by unusual flowers the color of fire. Its architecture, fifteenth-century English, looked to belong to a house of worship, but something about the door suggested it to be much older.

Wide, vertical lines streaked the door's wooden surface. They created branching pathways that went up and up, disappearing under the crimson foliage. An ornate ruby stone shone in the oily light—the door's knob. August's eye was drawn to it like a moth to flame.

He advanced forward. His footsteps unsteady. The mute men flanked him, seeming prepared to correct any misstep he might take. Dense bulbs weighted the vines along his path and burst open sequentially, blossoming in an explosion of flowers vibrant and as red as lava, but were velvet under his feet.

The closer he drew to the door, the more frenzied the

butterflies in his stomach became. Fear dizzied him, but his steps did not waver. When he came to stand directly in front of the door, the amalgamation of voices on the other side ceased. His chaperones broke off and stood at attention on opposite sides of the path.

August raised a hand to the blazing ruby gemstone. The words *danger* and *truth* came to mind. He couldn't stop himself even if he wanted to. The draw was too strong. He wrapped his fingers around the knob, turned it with unexpected ease, and the door opened inwards.

He crossed the threshold alone. The heavy door slammed shut behind him, but he was unphased by the clamor, distracted by the gaudiness he'd entered. The room was well-lit by golden lanterns, and the walls painted red from top to bottom. The ceiling was a crescent moon and the floor a setting sun.

Along the walls sat tables of varying sizes draped with fine gold and red linen. Above them hung gorgeous oil paintings. One painting, in particular, depicted unclothed women surrounding a buck under a clear night sky. Mounted just below each painting was a description placard. The placard under the painting of the women read *Of Red and White*.

What was this place? To August, the room was a mixture between a museum and a shrine. Behind him, where the door had been, there was none and no signs that one ever existed. He saw no other exit.

He approached a table. The one that called to him most hosted a glass display case lit from the inside. The case housed what appeared to be an ordinary but ruined piece of plank wood. Before the wood lay a sheet of equally ordinary paper, yellowed by age. The black ink used to chronicle the list he was looking at had dried ages ago.

He found the script handwriting difficult to read but not impossible. He strained his eyes. Stared so intensely at the manifest, the horns on his head raked the glass.

The header read Hall & Cargo Co. Ltd. Could it be? The very same company? The very same Hall & Freight Eva Barzaga had written about and died trying to expose?

August felt a sobering wariness breach his zombified state. The butterflies in his gut began to beat their wings again, and his skinny legs trembled. His palms, slick with sweat, pressed to the cool surface of the case as he skimmed the second line on the manifest. It read To and From East London, Algoa Bay, Cape Town and England.

He scrutinized passenger names. A solitary non-English name stood out from the rest: a male passenger listed as a servant named Kabunji. The name meant no more to him than the rest. They were all strangers. Ghosts on a page. But why would someone preserve a useless piece of wood? Let alone documents from a time people no longer cared about?

His eyes turned up to the painting hanging above the display. He could hear the storm as the RMS Dawn battled tumultuous ocean waves. The clipper ship's numerous ballooning sails were like clouds fleeing an oppressive and unforgiving sky. Hot white lightning pursued the vessel in dazzling streaks. Going by the placard, she fought the good fight from 1860 to 1872.

August covered the room end-to-end. He encountered South African artifacts, black and white photographs, and manuscripts with foreign text and symbols similar to astrology or alchemy. He didn't know which and comprehended neither.

The photograph at present rooted him in place. He watched a blistering inferno consume blurred stampeding cattle. What could only be bodies piled high smoldered in the background and black smoke rose off the corpses. He remembered what the trespasser had said. How she boasted about watching the shamans burn.

He tried to swallow the lump in his throat. He failed. His eyes wet as he felt a stirring in his stomach that wasn't butterflies but a sensation of slow waking.

He didn't get it. Why were tears streaming down his face? Why did he feel deeply hurt by the images? He hadn't known these people. They were relics of an unfortunate past that had nothing to do with him. Yet to think this way somehow felt wrong.

August glimpsed his reflection in the glass. Fixated his gaze seeing his blood-stained face and neck, the tall antlers, the pelt shrouding his nakedness. What was this place and why had he been brought here?

A whistling wind flitted the room. Like a blade, it cut the stale air introducing notes of sweet berries, wheat, and honey. August stepped away from the display and turned his attention in the direction of grinding stone. Seemingly without rhyme or reason, a section of wall drew into itself, a rectangular shape as tall and wide as an adult man. The opening, an impregnable ethereal blackness, looked to contain none and all the answers to his questions.

No warmth pacified his woes. His heart thundered with the

anxiety of a caged animal, but the door to his cage now stood wide open. It was his choice to step out, to leave the security the cage provided, and brave the unknown. The alternative was to stay where he was and let the onset hypothermia run its course. A piece of him felt it already had. Believed the ghostly warmth had only prolonged his unavoidable demise.

He glanced down at his fingers and saw they were a purplish blue. Drowsiness hung over him like a cloud. He looked back at the rectangular pit. The surrounding crimson made the yawning hole in the wall appear menacing, and August did not doubt that it was. The thought about there being things worse than death came to mind, but he needed to know.

He drew in a shaky breath, squeezed his eyes shut, and with a hand outstretched, like a blind man, he stepped into the black.

CHAPTER 23

THERE IT WAS AGAIN, THE aroma of ripe berries, wheat, and honey. On the other side of the wall, the scents had been delicate notes scattered on a mischievous wind. Here the sweet-smelling combination was a full-on ensemble. But aromatic or not, August was not seduced.

He waited, tense. He believed at any moment, he would be descended upon by guttural squawks and hisses and torn apart limb-by-limb. When his nightmare scenario did not play out, only then did he timidly open his eyes.

Grass replaced mosaic pavement, wet after a light rainfall. But how could there be rain when he was underground? He could smell it. And it wasn't the tainted kind of rainwater captured and transported by industrial drainpipes. What he smelled was fresh and earthy.

August lifted his eyes and beheld more impossibilities. The moon, for example. Not a painstakingly crafted mural as it had been in the red room, but a real celestial body newly born and radiating vitality. Its blue aura dominated a cloudless sky blanketed by a sea of stars.

The glowing rock was perfectly framed in the octagonal opening above. The encompassing exposed stone and brickwork evoked thoughts of his great-great-great grandfather's miniature castle. But unlike Braeden's castle, where he and his parents resided today, this place was in ruin, overtaken by nature and hollow.

August gravitated to the structure's center. He was being watched, trailed by turning stag heads resting on the shoulders of men. They were like well-dressed minotaurs standing at attention as they lined the interior walls forming a perfect octagon.

In addition to the black two-piece suits his silent chaperones wore, the onlookers sported black gloves, black aprons embroidered with gold, and black and gold sashes running from left shoulder to right. Around their necks on gold chains hung twin antler insignias. Each one had a varying number of points.

There were about twenty onlookers, if not more. August saw them but did not see them. His concentration laser-focused on what lay ahead. He felt a magnetic pull to it as his heartbeat quickened. A type of nauseating foreboding feeling that twisted his stomach in knots.

An altar, three feet in height and six in length shone brightly in the moonlight. Around it, wicker baskets overflowed with bushels of grapes while additional baskets contained wheat. The altar itself was almost completely covered in yellow and white honeysuckles. But none of these things contributed to August's elevated blood pressure. What sent his heart racing was on top of the altar.

A voice inside his head told him to stay away. He couldn't do that. He was here now, and there was no turning back. He came upon the altar, his legs heavy. An ominous presence arrested his breathing.

There she was, white as porcelain, and laid out on the altar like a Jane Doe in a morgue. Her face an enigma, shrouded by a white rabbit mask that was neither cute nor childish. Its red eyes, straw whiskers, and bucked teeth were unsettling. Her hair was cosmic fire.

"Do you remember when you were in the woods? You asked if I could hear you." said a man's voice at his back. Hands rested on August's shoulders. He stiffened. "I did. Every word. I know it was hard. It was hard for me too... that I couldn't help you any of the times I wanted to. The times you thought you needed me to."

"What is this?"

"Your rite of passage. A legacy started by your great-great-great-grandfather when he stepped foot off the RMS Dawn and onto English soil. He was one of the few shamans to escape Cape Colony. But the witches couldn't leave well enough alone. They pursued him. Because to them, one shaman is as dangerous as one hundred. But he was ready for them. Made a pact with the very deity they sought to destroy. Ninian the Lifegiver."

"Hail Ninian!" The onlookers erupted in solidarity.

August watched the subtle rise and fall of the woman's breasts. She was alive. "People died tonight. I almost died tonight." He said, sounding far away.

"Yes," Robert said. "That's part of who we are. Part of what this family is. Despite our means, a man must be able to stand on his own two feet. Tonight, you've done that. You chose to stand when anyone else in your position would have laid down and died."

"What were their names?"

"Names?"

"I can see their faces, but I can't remember their names. A butler. A bird."

"Does it matter? A man who murdered women and children. And a woman whose life was never her own."

August pondered his father's words. In some capacity, he thought it did matter. But not more than what he faced. Not more than the allure of the painted rabbit mask.

He reached a hand towards the woman, his fingers quaking as he wrapped them around the mask and lifted it. What he saw made him want to scream. He dropped the false face. A pitiful dry heave hunched his shoulders.

"Steady. Steady." Robert squeezed his arms.

August couldn't take his eyes off her. The vacant pale-green eyes, the beginnings of crow's feet at their corners, the tiny freckles no longer obscured by makeup, and raven black hair streaking a predominantly red mane. The world knew her as Veronica Foxx. August called her mother.

"Mother," He said. A simple word, but power on the lips

of a child, like evoking God. The man he called father moved beside him. August glimpsed him. Saw the great beast's head in place of his father's and the tall black antlers and their eighteen points. His regalia chain collar glistened. The emerald stones within the gold links shined with dull fire.

"This witch is not your mother." Robert said. "She is merely the vessel that brought you to us." His father took his hand. In it, he placed the white-handled knife that seemed to haunt August no matter where he went. "Braeden took their power. Their blood. Used it to integrate into modern society. He didn't want to at first but figured it a fool's errand to return to Cape Colony to play the hero."

August was at a loss for words. He gaped at his mother, the woman whom his father claimed to be a witch. The woman who had nursed him when he was a babe and watched over him in his father's absence.

"It takes more energy than one could imagine to break a person down completely." Robert continued, releasing the knife. August held it, his grip limp. "But a part of them always remains. Reemerging in moments of clarity. Do you see?"

His mind struggled to digest the man's words. Weariness stressed his face. He recalled numerous no-holds-barred clashes between his parents. Observed in silent horror how their arguments had devolved over the years from shouting matches to the one-sided merciless tirades his father would launch against his mother.

What had been most shocking was the man accusing the woman of being unfaithful and blaming August's recessive genes on her lying down with someone from the *lesser race*.

Before that day, he had never heard the man use the term, although there had been rumors of his father's prejudice.

It had infuriated August, made him think of the mixed girl in his class and how other students chose to ostracize her. And for what? Because she looked different?

Emboldened by righteous anger, he had intervened in his mother's tongue lashing. What followed was disheartening, and so unlike his mother, it had left him stunned. She had looked him straight in the eye and told him that everything bad in her life was because of him. Seeing her on the altar now brought understanding to the vitriol in her words. His eyes were wide open.

"While it's true our blood is unique, like bees to honey, those crones came for their sister." His father said.

"They brought it on themselves," spoke an older man. August felt cloth fingers wrap around his knife-wielding hand. A second beast's head appeared to his right, identical to his father's. "Everything you saw in that room is the truth. They set these events in motion. Whispered the words and weaved the spells that caused the betrayal and murder of our ancestors. But fate got the last laugh in the end. Because powerful men pay attention to history and leave no opportunity for the same shortcomings to befall them. So, what did these powerful men do? They began to exterminate witches like rats. Burned them at the stake as they had done our kin. Ran them out," The old man chuckled darkly.

Although slightly muffled, August knew his grandfather's voice well. He listened to his words as the man guided his hand to his mother's unclothed body, the knife an extension of his touch. He couldn't help but wonder if his mother's constant coddling and calling him rabbit had been an unconscious ploy to crush his independence. Even if it were, the revelation did not stop the tears streaking down his cheeks.

With the blade flat on its side, his grandfather continued to guide his hand, tracing an invisible line from Veronica's navel to her solar plexus. "We adapted." He said. "Chose to do more than survive. We thrived and will continue to thrive when it is your time to lead. However, we can no more make a choice for you than the god we serve. But to offer Ninian the blood of his enemy is a guarantee for a long and healthy life." He released August's hand, and the weight of the knife again became apparent.

"She helped me." August muttered.

"That's possible and likely. But are you certain the reason as to why were laudable? Without encouragement on our part?" Robert said.

August wasn't certain. The trespasser had said he was being protected, and up till now, he thought the *she* the trespasser had been referring to was another, the one whose face he could vaguely recollect but name he remembered not: the bird.

"And if I choose not to do this?" August asked.

"Your body has been pushed to its limits. It is by Ninian's grace that you can stand at all." His father said. "If you chose to forfeit your inheritance, you will pass from this world to the hereafter." The man confirmed what August knew deep down all along. It was true, then, that he teetered on the line between sleep and eternity, explaining why his toes, fingers, and lips hadn't regained their color.

His downcast eyes studied the face of the woman who

birthed him. She had been two women. One loved him unconditionally, and the other despised him. His whole life, he thought himself to be one thing, and the truth he found was gruesome on both sides.

On the one hand, his family's secret allowed them to move through society undetected. They had become one of the most powerful families in the Western world. The flipside was the road had been paved in blood, albeit the blood of an enemy he never knew existed.

August did not believe in karma, but the coincidence too big to ignore. The witches had influenced men to give in to their wickedness in exchange for power. Therefore, empowering themselves, although their ambitions were short-lived. Tonight, they had come to exact revenge on the vengeful. They killed his butler. They killed a bird. What were their names? Why couldn't he remember?

The fog grew thick over his brain and the big sleep closing in. His heart should've been jackhammering. It was slowing down. He was slowing down. His vision clouded with more than just tears as death lingered like a silent spectator.

The knife's bone handle slid between his clammy fingers. He was tempted, very tempted, to let gravity do its job and make the decision for him. If the knife hit the ground, it would stay there. Easy peasy lemon squeezy.

All eyes were on him. Shining stag eyes, expectant and sinister. His father and grandfather were the only ones close enough to notice his failing grip. True to their word neither made a move to do anything about it. At the last possible second, he clenched his fist so tight the handle's indentations dug into his palm. The pain jolted him and the decision made.

August raised the knife shakily. His mouth dry. His eyes flashed, homing in on the invisible line his grandfather had demonstrated.

Maybe this was all one big lie, an elaborate hoax for his sixteenth birthday. The type of Rockefeller shit only people like them could afford, and years later, they would look back and laugh. By then (if alive at all), he would be the permanent resident of a wheelchair, a catatonic thing left in a corner and occasionally checked on by the poor soul tasked to wipe the drool from his chin. Yes, that made sense. He'd stab his mother with the knife, the faux blade will retract, and everyone laughs.

August brought down the blade in an unremarkable way. It did not retract. He felt the skin resist but ultimately give way to the startling real sharpness and watched as bright red dots surfaced. He anticipated Veronica's mouth to open in a banshee's wail, and when she didn't scream, that was somehow more unnerving than if she had.

The knife didn't stop. It sank two then three inches deeper, and the bright red dots became a pool of blood in Veronica's navel that began to overflow. Darkness swept away the blue lunar light. When light returned, the moon was larger, and a deep vermillion hue baptized the castle ruins.

August felt sick. A manic kind of sickness that threatened to manifest as laughter. He thought about a southern American businessman he crossed paths with at a fundraiser. He had overheard the man bragging about a court victory. "My lawyers gutted that lawsuit from the rooter to the tooter," he had said.

He asked him what that meant, and the man had given him a skeptical look. The look all adults gave when deciding whether a youngster was trying to be a smartass or not. He decided that August was on the level, and with queer delight, had explained the intricacies of butchering hogs. Where the man came from, no parts of the hog went to waste. They used the whole hog from the rooter to the tooter.

August had laughed then and was laughing again now. A body-shaking, soundless laugh contradicting his bloodshot eyes and tear-stained cheeks.

The knife cut upwards on its predetermined route, a hand gripping his on either side. They steered him, father and grandfather, from puncturing any vital organs. The skin split apart and, the words played over and over again in the businessman's comical southern drawl. *From the rooter to the tooter* and *No parts go to waste.*

Just shy the solar plexus, the blade's journey ended. His father relinquished his hold. August did the same, although it was his father who pried open his fingers. His grandfather took dominion over the knife, extracted it.

For a man eighty-four years of age, his grandfather rounded the alter with a speed and surefootedness befitting a much younger man. August paid heed. A giddy spirit embraced him. The spirit's name was Retribution, and the years anchored to the Foxx clan had diluted its soul. While retribution was punishment inflicted on someone as an act of vengeance, it was uncharacteristic sadistic satisfaction that curled his lips in expectation of what was in store.

His grandfather thrust a hand inside the living, breathing sacrifice. A solitary tear leaked from Veronica's eye. Finding what he sought, he used the knife the way a hunter would on a fresh kill to harvest his prize.

Quick, decisive cuts freed what his grandfather wanted.

He plucked it out. Another slice and he peeled away the thin membrane covering the organ. A slick liquid soaked his gloves.

August's grin faded when the man offered it to him. He lifted his arms and cupped his hands together, accepting the hot organ within his palms; a human heart, the witch's heart, his mother's heart. It was heavy as most things to him were, and perhaps it should be because the moment itself was.

"In the eyes of Braeden!" His grandfather proclaimed. All under the sound of his voice repeated the words with the exclusion of August. "In the eyes of Ninian!" Their voices thundered, quaking stone and brick.

The pilot light in his belly, ignited by the truth of his family legacy, had become a blistering firestorm. His eyes boiled, glowering at the heart in his hands. He saw the shamans being burnt alive, cattle fleeing in terror, crops burning in a misguided and desperate sacrifice to call on the ancestors for liberation, the famine that followed.

"Take, eat; this is the body of His enemy." His father said.

"For the body of His enemy is our enemy. Their power is our power." The men raised their voices collectively and casually, like reciting a hymn. August brought the heart to his lips. He bit into it. Blood exploded in his mouth, releasing a pungent, bitter metallic taste. He forced down the knee-jerk reaction to throw up.

"Drink of it, all of it, for this is His enemy's blood, which is poured out for the many who died because of them," His father's words resonated.

He did not need to see to know he was under scrutiny by the onlookers. He felt their emotions; anger, joy, hopefulness, and fear. Everyone watching him expected the best but was prepared for the worst. He fixated on his grandfather, swallowed the contents in his mouth. He bit into the muscle again, felt his teeth sever tendons, chewed vigorously, and swallowed. He continued until nothing remained.

August's lips, no longer smacking, made way for uncomfortable silence. He resisted the urge to tongue the flesh stuck in his teeth. He felt ill. His stomach cramping. He thought someone would say something or do something, but no one said or did anything.

Behind his grandfather's head, a shadow grew dwarfing tall antlers. The shadow became branching curved spires stretching towards the open roof. Two heads above his grandfather's, the shadow stopped growing and solidified. Twin emerald spheres bobbed like buoys then settled. August was awe-struck.

Clopping hooves approached and his grandfather stepped aside. Twice now, he had laid eyes on the black stag. To look at its body was to stare into the abyss. To look in its eyes was to look into the infinite loop that was life and death.

He was not afraid. In contrast to their previous encounter, he was equipped with an insight he lacked before. He beheld the Lifegiver, Ninian. He beheld his great-great-great-grandfather, Braeden. Dual souls inhabiting one vessel.

The god bowed its crowned head. August reciprocated the act. The reason as to why, not an admirable one. His stomach knotted, burned like acid trying to eat its way through. He cradled his belly, doubled over, and narrowed his eyes then shut them completely.

RUN RABBIT RUN

The insufferable aching wrenched his bowels like a vice, his muscles convulsed, and saliva dribbled copiously out his mouth, hanging in thick frothy strands. He thrust his face to the moon, issuing a tortured shriek. His innards pushed, pulled, and rearranged. When he opened his eyes, they were a brilliant and haunting green. The stag threw back its head and roared.

EPILOGUE

8:00 a.m.

THE SNOW HAD STOPPED FALLING and the morning still. Parked in the drive sat a black and silver Ford F-150 and matching Ford Expedition. From left to right, starting at the rear passenger doors and ending at the front doors of either vehicle, read POLICE in bold silver letters. Underneath, in a smaller font, read CITY OF REDBREAST.

Sheriff James Kentrell hadn't touched his tea. Invited to the sitting room, he sat perched on the edge of a sturdy high-backed chair. His smooth brown face made him look younger than his forty-plus years of tenure walking God's green earth. However, his deep-set brown eyes insisted he'd seen more than he'd ever care to admit, and salt and pepper hair gave him away whenever he removed his wide-brimmed hat. He sighed and ran his fingers through his close-cut hair, which was overdue for a lineup.

"Firstly, as cliché as it sounds, I truly am sorry for your loss," Kentrell said. "With that said, your boy did the right thing by calling us. Had he called state patrol, this place would be a media circus, and there wouldn't be a damned thing we could do about it."

"August is a bright lad," Robert said. "Given the situation, I'm proud of him responding the way he did."

Kentrell nodded. He saw past the expensive clothes, manicured nails, and overpriced haircut. He wasn't looking at an astute businessman but at a father who had almost lost his son. He thought about his boy back home and prayed that he never experiences the feeling firsthand.

"How do you suggest we proceed, sheriff?" Robert inquired.

"Well, everything seems to line up with August's statement." Kentrell said, sparing the young man a passing glance. The boy sat nearest the fireplace rolling something between his index and thumb. He wore an expression of meditative contemplation. Kentrell's cop intuition took an interest.

"We got one body upstairs in the master bedroom," he started. "Another one outside at your fountain buried up to the neck in snow like some morbid take on Frosty the Snowman. Then there's the third out there in the woods half-frozen to the ground. Now that doesn't account for the girl my deputies found in the garage. She's related to the deceased butler, am I right?"

"Yes, that's correct," August said. "His niece. They rarely

got the chance to see each other, so my parents agreed for her to travel with us on holiday."

"Alright." Kentrell wet his lips. A young upstart would have pressed with more questions. Unsurprisingly, youth and being overzealous often went hand-in-hand. He had no aspirations of becoming FBI or CIA. He was content with being a small-town sheriff who busted up the expected domestic dispute. He was the dad who never missed his kid's youth wrestling exhibitions and the husband whose wife brought him his lunch whenever he forgot to snag the brown paper bag off the kitchen counter.

Principally, there was his understanding when it came to toppling dominos. You knock over one, they all fell. No, sir. He wouldn't be the man responsible for toppling the many lives in Redbreast dependent on the shortline rail and salt mines.

"The way I see it is a botched robbery. This place sits empty most of the year, right? So, it isn't farfetched at all to assume our aspiring robbers visited the house probably a handful of times before deciding to make a move. Not expecting to meet any resistance, they encounter your boy here and the butler. Things escalated from there." Kentrell said.

"Will this be in the papers?" Robert asked.

"Afraid so, Bobby. But I'll pull some strings." Kentrell said as if he weren't pulling enough strings already. "We got to give the public something; you know that. But don't worry. I'll make sure the grizzly details are toned down."

He stole another intuitive glance at August. The young man seemed unperturbed by the discussion, but Kentrell didn't think the kid was insensitive. It wasn't uncommon for people to have a delayed reaction to traumatic events. For some people, it hit a day later, for others a week, and in rare occurrences months. Thankfully the family matriarch hadn't been here for any of it. Safely tucked away overseas and oblivious to the whole thing.

"I suppose it can't be helped." Robert relented. "How long will it take to sort the matter? The premises, I mean."

Kentrell redirected his attention to the patriarch. "Already got a wrecker on the way. Coroner van, too." He decided to go with the more politically correct terminology instead of *meat wagon*. He leaned his bulk forward. The thin gold chain he wore daily and kept tucked away in his shirt spilled free over his collar. A big hand went to one knee, and with a grunt, he catapulted to his feet. "Oh, I say my people will have this mess cleaned up by noon. One o'clock at the latest. You've got my word on that."

"You have my complete confidence, Jamie." Robert stood. They shook hands.

Kentrell retrieved his hat from the armrest. "We take care of our own around here. Redbreast hasn't forgotten what your family's done for us. If it weren't for you and the Samsons, we'd be a ghost town. Just another dead and forgotten city on America's long list of dead and forgotten cities."

He started for the door, but curiosity got the better of him. When he turned around, August was already on his feet. The young man was straight up and down like a beanpole, his skin smooth and bone white, and his eyes, those green eyes, were bewitching. He was the spitting image of blue blood aristocracy.

"Say, young buck," Kentrell said. "What you got there isn't something I need to take a look at, is it?" He raised the question as he tucked the gold crucifix back down his shirt. The *something* he was referring to was the blue USB thumb drive that had the youth transfixed.

August appeared to weigh his query. True to form, like the few members in society who have a sense of self and are accustomed to answering to no one, he showed no urgency to reply. His fingers rapped along the mantle above the fireplace. With a flick of the wrist, the thumb drive was tossed into the flames.

The plastic bubbled, and within seconds, the flash memory popped. A few seconds more, the plastic began to whine, releasing a high-pitched squeal. To Kentrell, the sound was like voices, people crying out. In his head, they grew louder, distinct, and as a result, he almost missed what the young heir said.

"There are some rabbit holes you just shouldn't go down."

N.A. WILLIAMS

is a new voice in the occult horror fiction realm. To learn more about the author and stay up to date on upcoming projects, contests, and more, visit www.authornawilliams.com.

Made in the USA
Columbia, SC
06 October 2022

68762663R00150